DEAD MAN TALKING

A Cozy Paranormal Mystery

JANA DELEON

Welcome to Everlasting

Dead Man Talking Copyright © 2017 by Jana DeLeon

J&R Publishing

The Happily Everlasting Series

COZY PARANORMAL MYSTERY ROMANCE NOVELS

Dead Man Talking

by Jana DeLeon

Once Hunted, Twice Shy

by Mandy M. Roth

Fooled Around and Spelled in Love

by Michelle M. Pillow

Witchful Thinking

by Kristen Painter

Visit Everlasting

https://welcometoeverlasting.com/

About Dead Man Talking

A HAPPILY EVERLASTING SERIES NOVEL

Welcome to Everlasting, Maine, where there's no such thing as normal.

Meteorologist Zoe Parker put Everlasting in her rearview mirror as soon as she had her college degree in hand. But when Sapphire, her eccentric great-aunt, takes a tumble down the stairs in her lighthouse home, Zoe returns to the tiny fishing hamlet to look after her. Zoe has barely crossed the county line when strange things start happening with the weather, and she discovers Sapphire's fall was no accident. Someone is searching the lighthouse but Sapphire has no idea what they're looking for. Determined to ensure her aunt's ongoing safety, Zoe promises to expose the intruders, even though it means staying in Everlasting and confronting the past she thought she'd put behind her.

Dane Stanton never expected to see Zoe standing in the middle of her aunt's living room, and was even more unprepared for the flood of emotion he experiences when coming face to face with his old flame. Zoe is just as independent and determined as he remembered, and Dane knows she won't rest until Sapphire can return to the lighthouse in peace, so he offers to help her sort things out.

Armed with old legends, Sapphire's ten cats, and a talking ghost, Zoe has to reconcile her feelings for Dane and embrace her destiny before it's too late.

To Mandy M. Roth, Michelle M. Pillow and Kristen Painter...you know why.

Chapter One

Zoe Parker hurried into the hospital and up to the desk. "I'm here for Esmerelda Parker."

The nurse frowned and lifted her hands to the keyboard.

Zoe held in a sigh. "Sapphire. Sapphire Parker."

The nurse smiled. "Of course. You must be Zoe. I see the family resemblance. I'm Mary Josephine Harris, but everyone calls me Mary Jo. I'm a Texas transplant, but you probably figured that from the accent."

Zoe nodded. It had crossed her mind that Mary Jo didn't exactly sound like a local. Her poufy hair and big toothy smile were also dead giveaways. People from the north tended to be a bit more stoic. Maybe it was the cold.

"We didn't figure you'd be able to make it right

away, but I'm sure glad you did," Mary Jo said. "Your aunt's been raising a ruckus."

"I'm sure," Zoe mumbled.

Her great-aunt Esmerelda, who insisted on being called by her mystical name Sapphire, was an expert at raising a ruckus. It was probably embedded in her DNA. There was no end to the tales the fine people of Everlasting, Maine, could tell about Sapphire Parker, the crazy cat lady who lived in the old lighthouse and used an adult tricycle as her main form of transportation. Her backup "vehicle" was her Nikes, she liked to say.

But despite her many eccentricities, Sapphire held a special place in Zoe's heart. So when she'd received a call telling her that her aunt had fallen and was unconscious with a concussion, Zoe had made a hasty phone call to her employer and hopped on the next plane out of Los Angeles. Between the waiting, the flight, and the drive in the rental car, Zoe had spent eleven hours in commute. She was exhausted, starving to death, and in desperate need of a shower and a breath mint, but she wasn't going anywhere until she made sure her aunt was okay.

"She's in room 28," Mary Jo said, and pointed to the double doors to her right. "Visiting hours ended at nine, but I know you've been traveling a while. Go on back, but don't stay too long. She needs her rest."

Zoe started to ask the nurse for more details of her aunt's condition but decided against it. She could always ask on her way out. Better to head to her aunt's room now while Mary Jo was giving her a pass. If a doctor saw her, that leniency would probably be over. She thanked the nurse and passed through the double doors the nurse had indicated. The Intensive Care Unit lettering on the door made her tense up. Just how bad off was Sapphire?

She located room 28 and slipped inside. The overhead light was off, leaving only the soft light from the hospital bed to illuminate the room. Her aunt was propped up a bit, her head turned to the side. Her long wavy hair—dyed sapphire color— stuck out from her head in every direction, and her face was so pale that Zoe yanked her gaze to the heart monitor. If it hadn't been for the steady pulse moving across the screen, she would have thought her aunt had passed. She was so still.

Zoe stepped up to the side of the bed and felt a wave of guilt course through her. Sapphire had just turned eighty years old but she'd never looked her age. Even though she was pale and had dark circles under her eyes, her skin still looked like that of a much younger person. But looks were deceiving. Sapphire might appear younger, but the calendar didn't lie.

You should have visited her.

Zoe put her hands on the bed railing and

clutched the cold metal. When she'd first left Everlasting after graduating from college, Sapphire had asked every holiday for Zoe to come home and celebrate with her, like the old times. At first, it had been easy to say no. Zoe was a meteorologist, and the new person on the job always had to work holidays. It's not like the weather stopped changing so the entire staff could have time off.

So she'd worked holidays and spent her vacation time at workshops and conferences, pursuing certificates that said she was an expert in this and that. All so that she could get a promotion and be on the air. Working in the background, feeding all the cool weather information to the on-air personalities so that they could get all the credit and the glory, wasn't what Zoe aspired to. She loved the weather. Had been fascinated by it since she was a little girl, and more than anything, she wanted to share that passion with as many people as possible.

After a couple of years, Sapphire stopped asking and Zoe didn't have to make excuses anymore. Now she felt like the most awful person in the universe. She'd had Sapphire out to visit her as soon as she had an apartment and enough furniture to accommodate a visitor, and her aunt had loved the sunny weather and having breakfast at the pier and watching the surfers. But Sapphire loved her lighthouse in Everlasting more than any other place in the world, and Zoe had only managed to get her out of it for a visit to California that one time.

Her aunt stirred and her eyes fluttered, then they opened and she looked up at Zoe and smiled. "Zoe," Sapphire said. "You came."

"Of course I came."

Sapphire smiled. "If I'd known all it took was a fall down the stairs to get you back here, I would have done it a long time ago."

Zoe reached over and placed her hand on Sapphire's. "I should have come to visit before now. I'm sorry I didn't."

"Don't be apologizing. You have your own life to live. You're not responsible for the failing balance of an old lady. Besides, your mother and father swing up here once a month to make sure I haven't gotten any crazier than I already was."

Zoe's parents had retired four years earlier and made a mad dash to escape the cold winters they'd endured their entire lives, deciding that the tropical climate Connecticut offered was more to their liking.

That was it. All three of Sapphire's remaining family members, and they'd scattered like mice as soon as the opportunity had presented itself. At the moment, Zoe's parents were in Australia on a month-long vacation, which is why Zoe had sped off to the airport at a moment's notice. If she could handle everything, then there would be no reason to alarm her parents and interfere with their vacation —the first they'd had in over a decade.

"What happened?" Zoe asked.

"I don't remember," Sapphire said. "The last thing I recall is going to bed. I took my knitting up with me and turned on HGTV—what a lot of complainers on that channel—and the next thing I remember is waking up here this afternoon with a doctor telling me that my brain was swollen and I'd been unconscious for a while."

"They told me you fell."

Sapphire shrugged. "I guess so, but I don't know why I'd go downstairs without changing first. It's way too chilly for me to have been traipsing around in only my nightgown, and that's all I was wearing when they brought me in."

"Who found you?"

"Oh, uh, a contractor I hired to update the kitchen. He starts work early. I'm finally bringing that place into this century. Only the half bath downstairs to do after the kitchen, and the whole place is done. I left your bedroom the same but the rest is updated. You'll see. It's beautiful."

"It was beautiful already."

Sapphire smiled. "You always loved it there. I'm glad you're here. The lighthouse will be glad, too, and the cats. Don't let Cornelius bother you. He just likes to hear himself talk."

Zoe nodded but didn't say anything. She seriously doubted the lighthouse would care one way or the other if she paid it a visit, and the cats were happy to see anyone with opposable thumbs. Zoe had no idea who Cornelius was. Maybe her aunt had branched out into some other species of the animal kingdom. She just hoped it was something made for indoor living. When Zoe was in high school, Sapphire had made "friends" with a wild boar she'd named Harold. The living situation hadn't turned out well for her aunt, Harold, or the lighthouse. Sapphire's strange ideas about things had given her quite a reputation in the small seaside community, but rather than becoming offended, her aunt had always taken the offbeat comments as compliments.

Sapphire squeezed her hand, and then her arm slid to her side. Her eyes slowly closed and within seconds, she'd slipped off into a deep sleep. Zoe backed away from the bed, careful not to bump it, and left the room. Clearly, her aunt needed to rest, and Zoe needed to find someone who could tell her exactly what had happened.

Mary Jo flashed her a hundred-watt smile as she stepped into the reception area. "Was she awake?"

"She woke up when I got there," Zoe said. "We spoke for a bit, then she drifted off again. Can you tell me what happened? She seems a little confused about everything."

"She took a bit of a hit to the head when she

fell, and the doctor said there's still some swelling. Also, her heartbeat was off when she got here. Between the wonky heartbeat, the swelling, and the meds, it's no wonder she's not up to snuff, although it does seem like her pulse has stabilized."

"That's good, I'm sure, but what does it mean?"

"That the symptoms were likely due to the stress of the fall and probably not indicative of a bigger problem with her heart itself."

Zoe felt relief spread through her. Bruises would heal and the concussion would probably be all right. Heart problems were a whole different deal.

"She said she fell down the stairs but she was still wearing her pajamas," Zoe said. "She never leaves her bedroom without getting dressed. Did she say anything when the paramedics brought her in?"

Mary Jo shook her head. "She was unconscious when they arrived. I was here this afternoon when she woke up, and the doctor asked her a bunch of questions, but she couldn't remember anything. He said her memory might come back once the swelling goes down, but he can't guarantee it."

"How long had she been lying there before the contractor found her?"

"It's hard to say, but the doctor thinks maybe a couple of hours based on the bruising."

Zoe blew out a breath. "Thank you for letting me see her."

"You're family. I know rules are rules and all,

but sometimes breaking them is more important than keeping them. Sapphire needed to see you. She'll sleep better and recover faster knowing you're here taking care of her home and her babies."

"What time do visiting hours start tomorrow?"

"Ten a.m. Dr. Prescott has been taking care of Sapphire since he moved here a couple years ago. He's old-school and does home visits. A lot of the older patients love that, especially the ones who don't drive. He's overseeing her care here and will be making rounds when visiting hours start. You can talk to him then."

"Great. Have a good night."

"You too, honey."

Zoe headed to her car and pulled out of the parking lot, directing the vehicle to the road that led straight through downtown and then out to the decommissioned lighthouse that Sapphire and her untold number of cats called home. Sapphire's babies. The last time Zoe had talked to her aunt, she said she was "down" to eight. Eight didn't sound like a "down" sort of number to Zoe, but then with her schedule, she couldn't even keep a cactus alive.

As she drove, she processed everything her aunt and Mary Jo had told her, but no matter how many times she rolled the facts over in her mind, she still didn't like them. Something didn't make sense. Other people probably wouldn't think twice about her aunt proceeding downstairs in her pajamas, but

Zoe knew better. Even if the past six years had decreased the sharpness of Sapphire's mind, surely decades of doing the same thing held more weight.

If her aunt had gotten up before daylight and gone downstairs without putting on her "walking clothes" as she called them, then there had to be a reason. And it wasn't a simple one. Because the master bedroom was on the third floor and the stairs were narrow and wound around in a somewhat steep circle, Sapphire maintained a small refrigerator in her bedroom. So there was no need to fall down the stairs in pursuit of something to drink in the middle of the night. She even had a Keurig on her desk for the days when she felt like having a cup of coffee and watching the sea before she went downstairs to make breakfast.

Her meds were located in her bedroom or the kitchen, depending on what time they were taken, and she kept first aid and things like cough syrup and drops in both rooms. This arrangement allowed Sapphire to go up and down the stairs only once a day. Her aunt had lived that way for longer than Zoe had been alive. Unless Zoe arrived at the lighthouse and things were completely different, then she was going to operate under the assumption that something out of the ordinary had gotten her aunt out of bed and on her way downstairs.

And Zoe wasn't leaving until she found out what had happened.

THE WOODS outside of town were denser than Zoe remembered, the trees seeming to come right up to the edge of the road, making her feel like the foliage was closing in on her. Storm clouds circled overhead, leaving the light from her headlights the only illumination in the otherwise pitch black, and she clenched the steering wheel, her anxiety over her aunt's injuries and the impending storm increasing as she went. She'd slowed to a crawl when she rounded a corner and a burst of lightning lit up the sky, exposing the lighthouse that rose up in front of her.

Zoe had always thought the lighthouse was one of the coolest places she'd ever seen, but with the backdrop of the oncoming storm, it looked somewhat ominous and slightly ethereal. She shook her head. She'd managed two decades in Everlasting without buying into the fanciful ideas that her aunt and many of the townsfolk held. Exhaustion, worry, and hunger pangs weren't about to send her over that edge.

She pulled up in front of the imposing tower and parked as close to the front door as the flower beds allowed, barely managing to get onto the porch with her backpack before the onslaught of rain began. She stood under the tiny awning and thought wistfully of the fuzzy pajamas that were in her suitcase in the trunk, but no way was she taking the time to retrieve the suitcase in the monsoon. She'd be soaking wet and freezing besides.

She dug the key out of her backpack, unlocked the door, and hurried inside as a huge gust of wind forced a sheet of rain under the awning. She had to shove the door a bit to get it shut with the wind working against her, but finally she got it locked and reached for the light switch. She flipped it on but nothing happened.

Great.

She pulled her cell phone out of her pocket and turned on the flashlight to guide her through the living room and into the kitchen. She flipped the light switch in the kitchen but still nothing happened. The power must be out because of the storm. She'd forgotten that part about the lighthouse. Even a gentle spring rain tended to kick the power off.

Her stomach had been rumbling for the past hour, the package of peanuts she'd eaten on the plane worn off long ago. She'd intended to find something to eat when she got to her aunt's house, but now the thought of poking around for food and eating in the dark just made her feel even more exhausted. Even the hot shower she'd been looking forward to seemed like a whole bunch of effort.

Using her phone, she made her way up the first section of the winding staircase to the second floor.

There was a small landing with two doors, then the stairs continued up to her aunt's room on the third level of the lighthouse. Because the lighthouse began to narrow as it rose, nothing was constructed beyond the third level. After that, the stairs continued up to the top of the lighthouse tower where the light used to guide ships safely back to port.

The door to the left led into what was charitably considered a bunk room. When her aunt purchased the lighthouse, it had contained two sets of bunk beds built into the walls on each side. It had the appearance and claustrophobic feeling of being in a submarine. Her aunt had torn out the beds and turned the small room into a decent-sized closet. The door on the right led to the room her aunt had dubbed Zoe's room. The sleigh bed was still on the front wall, offering a full view of the picture window across from it. Lightning flashed across the sky, illuminating the small space, and in that moment of brightness, Zoe could tell that nothing had been changed. The room was exactly as it was six years ago when she'd left for California.

It was both comforting and sad. Comforting that her aunt had kept the room here just for her and sad that she hadn't bothered to change it for her own use. She tossed her backpack onto the bench at the end of the bed and pulled off her shoes and jeans. When this crisis was over, things were going to change. From now on, Zoe was going to make the time to visit at least once a year, even if she used precious vacation time to do it. Jobs would come and go, but she only had one Aunt Sapphire and she wasn't going to be around forever. This fall was a stark reminder of that fact.

She pulled back the covers and climbed into the bed, propping herself up a bit with the pillows so that she could watch the storm. The thunder boomed so loud that it shook the walls, and the lightning flashed so brilliantly across the sky that it was momentarily blinding. Finally, the lightning stopped and all that remained was the downpour. She felt her eyes grow heavy and before she knew it, she was nodding off to the rhythmic sounds of the pouring rain.

The slumped position she'd fallen asleep in resulted in her head lolling to one side. Finally, her neck had enough of it and awakened her. She checked her watch, surprised that she'd been asleep in that position for a solid three hours. Lightning once again flashed in the distance, and the steady rain sounded against the window. She threw the covers back and headed for the bathroom, groaning when she flipped the light switch and got no response. The power was still out.

Her phone was back on the nightstand in her room, but the toilet was in between the shower and the vanity. Surely she could find it. She reached her hands out in front of her and finally connected with the toilet tank and the edge of the toilet lid, which was already up. She turned around and prepared to sit but as she lowered herself, the cold plastic she'd expected her exposed tush to connect with was furry and warm, and more importantly, angry.

She bolted upright as the cat yowled, hissed, and raked a claw across her bare bottom. She could hear its claws on the floor as it scrambled out of the room. What the hell? Sapphire told her the cats always hid during a storm. Sitting on the edge of an open toilet wasn't the kind of hiding Zoe thought a cat would opt for.

Her butt smarting from the scratches, she half limped, half shuffled back into the bedroom to get her phone. No way was she attempting that again without light. Given the intensity of the stinging, she might be sleeping on her side the rest of the night.

She sighed. It wasn't the least bit surprising that her return home had already become a huge pain in the rear.

Chapter Two

Zoe awakened the next morning to a glare of sun in her eyes. She groaned and pulled a pillow over her head. How could she have forgotten that the bedroom window faced east, looking out over the ocean? Maybe because her studio in LA faced west and she usually slept with a gel mask.

She tried to force her mind back to rest, but it was no use. God's spotlight, as her aunt called the sun, had brought her out of her slumber and there was no returning. She threw the covers back and rolled out of bed, then padded into the tiny bathroom. She flipped the wall switch and was happy when the overhead light popped on. Because of the remote location and frequent outages, Sapphire had installed a generator, but Zoe hadn't fired it up in years and was happy she wasn't going to have to depend on fuzzy recall to get it running.

While she was giving silent thanks for the restored power, she looked around the remodeled bathroom. Even in the dark, it had felt different the night before, but the tiny glimpses she'd gotten with lightning flashes hadn't revealed much. And after the whole butt-scratching-cat affair, she hadn't felt like retrieving her phone for a closer look. Now she blinked and looked around.

Sapphire hadn't been lying when she said she was bringing the house up to date. The bathroom was only large enough to contain sink, toilet, and shower, but the old lopsided, cheap wood cabinet had been replaced with a gleaming white porcelain pedestal sink. The floor was rid of the hideous yellow vinyl that had resided there since the dawn of time and was now covered in white marble tile with a turquoise vein running through it. The plastic shower stall was long gone, and the same tile on the floor made up the sides and bottom of the new shower with a glass door. The walls were painted light turquoise to match the vein in the marble. The entire effect made the room feel larger and relaxing at the same time.

As she splashed her face with cold water, she mulled over the generator situation, finally deciding it would probably be a good idea to figure it out in case another storm rolled through tonight. Not that Zoe minded sitting in the dark. She'd never had fanciful ideas about monsters under the bed or in the closet, but she knew Sapphire usually kept a well-stocked freezer, and too much downtime could spoil the goodies she had stored. And she definitely wasn't looking for a repeat performance with that cat.

As she stepped out of the bathroom, she saw something move in the hallway. Aside from her bathroom stalker, Zoe hadn't seen or heard the cats during the night and assumed they were hiding from the storm. But with the sun shining bright, they'd probably crept out from under furniture and were going about their regular cat business. She moved into the hall to see which of Sapphire's four-legged roomies was on the move and sucked in a breath.

It wasn't a cat. It was a man.

An old man with silver hair, wearing a white dress shirt, navy suit coat, and baby-blue-and-red plaid boxers. And he was going down the stairs.

She hurried back into the bedroom, shut the door, and locked it.

Think.

She pulled out her cell phone and started to dial 911. Then she stopped. Certainly the man couldn't be the contractor her aunt had mentioned, but what if he was one of Sapphire's friends? What if her aunt had asked him to stop by and check on things? Zoe had told the admitting nurse that she'd get there as soon as possible, but no one was expecting her last night. Sapphire might have made arrangements for the cats once she woke up.

Granted, the man had been wearing a suit coat and boxers, but that only gave more merit to the theory that he was a friend of Sapphire's. If he were there to rob the place, surely he would have put on pants. Men walking around in a suit on top and boxers on bottom would attract attention, even in Everlasting.

Sapphire didn't have any weapons that Zoe was aware of, unless you counted kitchen knives, and in order to get to those she'd have to go right past the man on the stairs. Zoe had Mace in her suitcase, but it was still in the car. She scanned the room, looking for something solid and easy to grip. Surely she could take down one old man if she needed to, right?

She glanced up at the oars hanging on the wall above the headboard. Sapphire used them for decoration, but Zoe remembered Sapphire telling her that she'd found old kayaks in the storage shed when she moved in. The kayaks couldn't be saved, but Sapphire had kept the oars to hang inside. They were solid wood.

Before she could change her mind, she lifted one of the oars from the hooks holding it in place and eased the bedroom door open. There was no sign of the man on the stairs, so Zoe slipped outside the room and began to creep down the stairs, hesitating every time a step creaked. When she got to the bottom, she paused and heard movement coming from the other side of the wall in the kitchen. She lifted the oar up like a bat, clenching it with both hands, and readied herself to spring around the corner and into the kitchen.

One. Two. Three.

Heart pounding, she whirled around the wall, eyes darting across the room, looking for the old man. But the male specimen standing in the middle of the kitchen and looking at her with a somewhat amused expression, wasn't even remotely similar to the man she'd seen on the stairs.

Dane Stanton had always been a prime example of how rugged men should look. Unfortunately, in the time Zoe had been gone, that hadn't changed. He was every bit as gorgeous and sexy now as the day he'd dumped her.

Zoe lowered the oar and glared at him. "What the hell are you doing in my kitchen?"

He gave her that grin that had always been impossible to resist. "Good to see you too. To answer your question, it's not your kitchen, and I'm here working."

He waved a hand around and Zoe realized that the room was in the midst of a remodel and he was holding a piece of tile. The walls had been painted, and beautiful seafoam-green cabinets with glass fronts had been installed, but the countertop, backsplash, and flooring were currently missing. As were appliances. It was a good thing she opted to skip that meal last night. She'd have been highly disappointed if she'd had the energy and desire to whip something up and had gotten a good look at the kitchen the night before.

"You're doing the remodel?" she asked.

"You sound surprised. If you remember correctly, I was always good with my hands."

A flush crept up her neck and she tried to will it back down before it hit her face, but it was no use. Her cheeks grew warm and his grin got bigger.

"I thought you were running one of the fishing boats for your dad," she said.

"I did for a bit, but I've always known it wasn't for me. Willie Cramer was getting up there in age and needed some help with his contracting business, so I thought I'd give it a try. Five years later, Willie retired and I took over."

"That's great. I mean, that you found something you really enjoy. Most people don't."

"You did."

She nodded but looked off at the cabinets behind him, unable to meet his gaze. Her choice of career hadn't been the wedge that had divided them, but her desired location for doing the job had been. Zoe had attended college with one thing in mind—to get out of Everlasting and have the kind of life she saw others living on television. The pull of the big city was too much for her to ignore. Fancy restaurants, designer boutiques, concerts, museums, art galleries, and so many people to choose friends from that it would be impossible to get stuck listening to a bore.

Everlasting was exactly the opposite. The same few eating places that had been there for fifty years, with menus just as old. The same people doing the same things they'd done every day and teaching their kids to do those things as well. It was like the entire place was on some big loop, repeating itself with every generation. And that wasn't even taking into account the odd things the good citizens of Everlasting believed as the gospel. Things most people thought about only when reading fictional stories about witches and ghosts.

"So how is LA?" he asked.

"Good. Busy. I've been working a lot of hours, trying to position myself for that big promotion that's opening up soon."

"Prime-time weather girl?"

It was so much more than the way he made it sound, which was almost immature and dismissive, but she knew better than to argue with him over it. They'd had this same argument so many times before and it always ended the same way. He didn't understand why being on television in Maine and talking about how the weather would affect fishing today couldn't be enough for her, and she didn't understand why he knew there was a huge, awesome world beyond the city limits, but had no desire to explore it.

She nodded, hoping that was the end of it, then moved to change the subject. "Did you do the remodel on the bathroom in my room?"

"I've done all the remodeling in the lighthouse. I hire a couple helpers when I'm working on a strict deadline, and I sub out anything but basic plumbing and electrical, but when the homeowner isn't in any hurry, I prefer to do the work myself. It's satisfying to see your artistic vision slowly turn into the thing you'd only previously imagined."

She blinked. Of all the things she'd expected from Dane Stanton, becoming a contractor wasn't one of them. Considering himself an artist was even higher on the list. Not that she disagreed with him. People who could look at anything tired and old and envision something modern and beautiful were definitely artists. It's just that in all the years she'd known Dane, basically her entire life, she'd never heard him express an interest in anything that way.

"Well, it's beautiful," she said. "The white and turquoise is serene and perfect for such a small space. I'm surprised Sapphire didn't redo the bedroom as well."

"I think she wanted you to pick things out. She held up on the work in the bathroom until it sprung a leak."

"Oh." Instantly, Zoe felt guilty. "Well, I'm looking forward to seeing the rest of the work you've done here."

He blinked, clearly surprised, but she could tell the compliment pleased him. "You didn't see it last night?"

"It was really late by the time I got here, and the power was out."

"I should have figured. Doesn't take much to shut it down, and that storm was a good one. Did you go by the hospital before you came here?"

His question held a tiny bit of reproach and Zoe instantly resented it. It was one thing for her to come down on herself for not visiting often enough —or at all, as the case may be—but it was entirely another thing for someone else to insinuate she wasn't living up to her responsibilities.

"I went straight from the airport to the hospital," she said. He could hardly find fault with that.

"How was she?"

"Awake, but weak. She fell asleep again quite quickly, but she sounded normal."

"Did she remember what happened?"

Zoe frowned. "No. I was going to ask you about that. You're the one who found her?"

He nodded. "I came in around seven. It was a little earlier than my usual time, but Sapphire gets up before sunrise so she never cared if I went at it sooner than planned. I walked through the kitchen, assessing the placement of the new light fixtures that I needed to order, and almost tripped over her."

"Where was she exactly?"

He pointed to the stairs. "Right at the bottom. Sorta laid out across the floor from the last step."

She looked down at the floor, as if expecting answers to materialize. "Here?"

He stared at her for a moment and smiled. "Going to play detective? I remember when you went through your Nancy Drew phase."

"I'm not channeling Nancy Drew or any other PI. I'm just trying to figure out what happened. What Sapphire said doesn't make sense."

"In what way?"

"She doesn't remember coming downstairs, and she was still wearing her nightclothes. Sapphire never leaves her bedroom without putting on her walking clothes. Not even the time that frayed cord on her blow-dryer caught the bathroom on fire. So unless you're going to tell me that Sapphire's personality or mental faculties have been drastically altered since I've been gone, I have to wonder what would have made her come downstairs without taking the time to change."

Dane frowned. "Sapphire is having a bit of stiffness in her lower back and knees. Probably arthritis, but her mind is as sharp as it's always been."

"Well, that stairwell winds around with landings on all three floors. She hardly slipped at the top and fell all the way into the kitchen. She came down those stairs for some reason, and I'd like to know what it was."

He turned his hands up. "I can't imagine what. If there was a noise, it would likely be one of the cats. They've been poking around at my construction stuff since day one. The door was locked when I came in, but I still called the police right after I called the paramedics. Just in case."

"They didn't find anything?"

"No forced entry. All doors and windows locked." He cocked his head to one side. "Is that why you jumped into the kitchen, ready to bash me with an oar?"

Suddenly Zoe remembered the man. "I thought I saw something moving on the stairs," she said, unwilling to describe exactly what she'd seen. Maybe it was fatigue or acute hunger making her see things.

"Probably one of the cats."

She nodded, not wanting to delve deeper into the discussion. "Sapphire said that I shouldn't let Cornelius's chatter bother me. Is he new? Or is she trying something besides cats?"

Dane shook his head. "I've only seen cats. I don't know of one named Cornelius, but it could be a nickname she has for one of them."

"I'm almost afraid to ask, but how many?"

"Ten right now."

Zoe turned to look into the living room. "Where are they, anyway?"

"The laundry room," Dane said. "Sapphire usually feeds them first thing in the morning and again at night, so I doled out their usual feast. They'll be scattered around here sleeping the rest of the day."

"And prowling all night. I got a surprise last night when I attempted a bathroom run in the dark. Apparently one of them was hiding on the toilet." She left out the part about almost sitting on the cat, and no way was she telling him about her rear bumper injury. It was bad enough she was standing there in wrinkled clothes and zero makeup. She wasn't even wearing a good push-up bra.

"The cat wasn't hiding there," Dane said. "It was probably using the restroom."

She blinked. "And by using you mean…"

"All the cats are toilet-trained. Gave me a start the first time I walked in on one, but it's amazing really. Not to mention a big savings on litter, smell, dust, and the time it takes to deal with all that."

"She potty trained the cats. You're not kidding me?"

He shook his head. "They even flush."

"Wow. Well, I'm going to leave a flashlight on the nightstand from now on. I really don't want to start a fight with a cat over the use of the bathroom."

"Probably a good plan. So how long are you staying?"

The question was innocent enough, but something about his tone made Zoe wary. It sounded a little too personal. The question was, did he want her to stay or was he hoping she'd clear out quickly?

"I'm not sure," she said. "I have to talk to the doctor this morning and get an idea of what Sapphire's recovery time might be. I don't want to contact my parents unless things get worse."

"Is anything wrong?"

"No. They're on vacation. Australia. They've been dying to go forever, and I don't want them to cut their plans short unless there's no other choice. Depending on how quickly Sapphire's recovery is expected to be, it might be necessary to arrange some in-home care until she's back to a hundred percent."

"And that's not something you can handle," he said, his tone disapproving.

"I have a job in another state and a promotion that I'm this close to getting and that three other people are vying for. The longer I'm away, the easier it is to promote someone else."

"I understand," he said, but his tone implied he didn't understand at all. "As you've probably noticed, the kitchen is not really usable. I moved the refrigerator into the laundry room, so you still have plenty of cold storage. Sapphire has been cooking on the grill on the patio. It has a hot plate for a skillet or pot. I know it's not ideal, but the appliances aren't going to arrive for another day or two."

"I can make do. I'm not a big cook anyway. Well, I better get changed. I want to be at the hospital when Sapphire's doctor makes his rounds."

She headed back upstairs, and that's when she remembered that her luggage was still in the trunk of her rental. The keys were in her bedroom, but if she went back downstairs for the suitcase, Dane would insist on carrying it up for her. And that wouldn't work at all. Standing across the kitchen from him had been hard enough. No way did she want to share the enclosed space of the bedroom with him. Even for only a few seconds.

She'd thought college and her job and moving across the country had cured her of her attraction to him. She was wrong.

DANE WATCHED as Zoe drove away, all the old feelings he'd stuffed down deep in his gut now stirring around and giving him an ache. Unfortunately, the ache wasn't located in his stomach. He'd figured the hospital would contact Zoe's parents. After all, they lived reasonably close and visited regularly. He hadn't known they were continents away.

When he'd pulled up that morning and seen a

car he didn't recognize parked out front, the thought had flashed through his mind that it might be Zoe, but he'd dismissed it in favor of the far more likely concept that her parents had simply bought a new car he hadn't seen yet. When she'd stepped into the kitchen, he felt as if someone had sucker punched him.

Even with wrinkled clothes, no makeup, and her long brown hair pulled back into a ponytail, she was still the most beautiful woman he'd ever known. Zoe thought she had to go above and beyond to get a prime television spot, but Dane figured if the producers couldn't see what he did, then they were too stupid to deserve her. Despite her obvious worry about missing too much work, Dane had every reason to believe that if Zoe wanted that spot, it was hers to turn down.

Although he'd been momentarily taken aback by her presence, the old frustrations—his comfortable defense mechanism—had kicked in and he'd grown more disappointed in the conversation as it continued rather than surprised by it. No matter, though. He was used to disappointing and frustrating interactions with Zoe. In some ways, it was comforting to know he still had that wall between them to step behind when he didn't want to deal.

He picked up a piece of floor tile and measured it. The easy answer would be to delay the work until Sapphire returned from the hospital, but he didn't really want to do that. For one, Sapphire loved to bake and was depending on him to give her the kitchen of her dreams. And even if he could come up with a good excuse for halting construction, she'd see right through it. The last thing he wanted was to get in a discussion with Sapphire about his past with Zoe.

He cut the tile and carried it into the kitchen to check the fit on the floor along the cabinets, then grabbed his trowel and set the tile into place. When he was done, he rose and stared at the floor where he'd found Sapphire and frowned.

The worst part about the conversation he'd had with Zoe was the questions she'd asked about her aunt's fall. Dane didn't know anything about Sapphire's living habits, especially her nighttime ones concerning dress, but Zoe did. Her insistence that her aunt wouldn't have gone downstairs before changing was troubling. If Sapphire had indeed broken a lifetime of habit to go downstairs in the middle of the night, then it must have been for a reason.

But what?

He stepped over to the bottom of the stairs and looked up, frowning. The cats probably prowled around at night, but Sapphire was used to that. A little racket among her four-legged friends wasn't likely to get her out of bed in the middle of the night, and even if it did, why weren't the lights on?

He'd forgotten to mention that to Zoe when he'd described how he found Sapphire, and now that he remembered, it bothered him. There was no storm that night and Dane hadn't seen a flashlight anywhere. Certainly Sapphire knew her own house, but even someone who'd climbed those stairs a million times would be foolish to take on the narrow, winding climb in the dark.

He thought about the position of her body on the floor and tried to remember where her hands were. Then he crouched down and looked into the living room. He rose again and headed for the couch, tilting it from the back all the way over onto the floor. There were two things underneath—a penlight and a can of Mace.

He put the couch back into place and sat down on it, clutching the two items in his hand. Zoe was right. Something had scared Sapphire enough to send her downstairs in the dark with Mace. But what? Or who? And was Sapphire the target, or was there something inside the lighthouse besides the owner that the intruder was interested in?

And if he didn't find it, was he coming back?

He rose from the couch, placing the penlight and Mace on the coffee table. As soon as Zoe got back, he'd show her the items. A sheriff's deputy had already been out once to review the scene, but given this new evidence, Zoe might want to ask them to make another visit. In the meantime, he was going to check all the windows in the lighthouse to make sure they were secure, then he was going to change all the locks.

No one was going to mess with Sapphire or Zoe in their own home.

Chapter Three

Zoe pulled into the hospital parking lot at five minutes till ten. She'd rummaged around in her room and found an old T-shirt that wasn't horribly wrinkled, then she'd taken a long shower in the new bathroom and put on her jeans from the day before and the old T-shirt and managed to get out of the lighthouse while Dane was out back cutting floor tile. A lost luggage experience had taught her to carry a spare pair of undies in her backpack, so things weren't as bad as they could have been.

The weather report was already calling for another rainy night, but hopefully the storm would hold off until Dane left for the day. Then Zoe could get her suitcase up to the bedroom without help. She knew she was being absolutely silly about the entire thing. Even if things went well with her aunt, she'd probably be in town for at least three days or more. She couldn't spend all of her time at the hospital, because they wouldn't allow it and Sapphire needed her rest. That left her with the options of staying closed up in the lighthouse with Dane or heading into town for a dose of local crazy. Neither option had her heels clicking, but she'd figure it out later.

Now she needed to talk to the doctor about Sapphire.

The nurse at the front desk was a dour older woman who could have taken lessons from the cheerful Mary Jo. She asked Zoe who she was, then requested ID and gave her the side-eye when she saw it was issued by the state of California. Finally, she jotted the license number down on a pad of paper and waved Zoe back. She figured the battle-ax was calling the sheriff's department for a background check as soon as she left the reception area.

Sapphire was awake when Zoe entered the room and sitting upright in front of a tray that was probably supposed to be breakfast but looked like gray stuff in varying textures. Sapphire looked as thrilled by the contents of the tray as Zoe did, but she beamed when she saw Zoe enter the room.

"I'm surprised to see you this early," Sapphire said. "You were never a morning person."

Zoe wasn't certain that being awake and fully clothed at 10:00 a.m. constituted being a morning person, but her aunt considered anyone who slept past 8:00 a.m. a slacker. If Zoe had her way, she would have slept every day until ten and stayed up until midnight. It's why she was gunning for the evening weather slot.

Zoe walked over and kissed her aunt on the forehead. "I wanted to be here when your doctor came by. What's this?" She gestured to the tray.

Sapphire wrinkled her nose. "Jury's still out on that one. They claim it's eggs and hash browns, but it doesn't look like any eggs and hash browns I've ever seen. On the plus side, if they don't plan on serving anything better they'll have to let me out before I starve."

Zoe smiled. It was typical of her aunt to find the silver lining in everything, even if it meant making a joke about it. The hospital had a policy against outside food but that was easy enough to get around.

"Unless they have you on a restrictive diet," Zoe said, "I'm sure I can arrange for some contraband meals."

"That's what I've always loved about you—your willingness to break the rules when they're stupid. How are you this morning? Did the storm knock out the power?"

"It did, but I was so tired I just crawled into bed. It was back on this morning."

"And the cats?"

"They were all hiding last night but Dane fed them this morning in the utility room. He said that was your usual routine."

Sapphire nodded. "He's a good boy. Talented, too."

"I haven't had a chance to see all the remodeling, but the bathroom in my room is beautiful, and the kitchen looks like it's going to be gorgeous. You must have been channeling me when you picked everything."

"Oh, I didn't pick it. Dane did. I just approve it and write checks. More work off my plate. He's really got an eye for that sort of thing. That's why I hired him."

"Yeah, about that…how come you didn't tell me he was the contractor you hired? And no fibbing. You hesitated last night when I asked you who found you. Now I know why."

Sapphire sighed. "I was afraid if I told you Dane would be there that you'd stay at the motel and I didn't want that. I know it's selfish, but the lighthouse needs family staying there. Dane is a nice young man, but he's not family."

Zoe knew Sapphire had strange ideas about the mystical power of the lighthouse. She told everyone who would listen about the strong positive energy she'd felt the instant she'd stepped inside the structure as a little girl. She'd known then that one day, it would be her place. She claimed it called to her when she was away.

Zoe wasn't one to buy into fanciful ideas like the kind Sapphire lived by, but she would admit that the lighthouse had a soothing effect on her. Something about it just felt right, but Zoe assumed that was because of the happy childhood memories she had that featured the lighthouse and Sapphire. Not because the lighthouse held some sort of power that couldn't be seen.

As Zoe contemplated what to say, a doctor with silver hair and tired eyes walked in and smiled at Sapphire.

"Ms. Parker," he said. "It's good to see you up and alert. How are you feeling this morning? Did you sleep all right?"

"Once I knew my niece was here," Sapphire said, "I slept like a baby. And I feel great. A little banged up, of course, but no more than a tumble down the walkway to the beach would get me."

"Well, maybe you should forgo walks down to the beach for a bit," the doctor said. He turned to extend his hand to Zoe. "I'm Dr. Prescott. You must be Ms. Parker's niece."

"Yes. I'm Zoe." She shook his hand. "How is she doing? Do you have more tests to run?"

"I want to take another scan of her head this afternoon. You can't be too careful with head injuries, but otherwise, she's in good shape considering. I imagine she'll be sore for quite some time, but it's a miracle she didn't break anything."

Sapphire frowned. "This afternoon? Why can't you scan it now? I want out of this joint."

"I'm afraid I can't release you just yet," Dr. Prescott said. "I want that swelling to go down before we talk about that. I suggest you get comfortable and watch television or read books. It's going to be a couple more days before I even consider giving you a clean bill of health."

"A couple more days?" Sapphire's voice went up several notches and Zoe placed a hand on her aunt's shoulder, trying to prevent her from going off on the good doctor. Normally, her aunt was one of those peace-loving hippie sorts, but if she was set on something and you got in her way, a whole different person emerged.

"Dr. Prescott is right," Zoe said. "He needs to make sure your brain is okay. It's not exactly a five-minute drive from the lighthouse to the hospital."

Sapphire sighed. "I wouldn't want to cause any more drama than I already have. I guess I can stick around here a bit longer."

Her aunt glanced at the tray of gray food, then back at Zoe. The message was clear. Sapphire would stay put as long as Zoe smuggled her in some real food.

"Is there anything she should avoid?" Zoe asked. "I was thinking of picking up her favorite cookies at the Witch's Brew Coffee Shop this afternoon."

"She has no dietary restrictions," the doctor said. "Her favorite cookies sound like just what the doctor ordered, and the baked goods at Witch's Brew would tempt even the strictest of dieter. Just don't let the charge nurse catch you with them. She's a real stickler for the rules." He patted Sapphire on the arm. "You're in good hands. I'll see you after the scan."

Sapphire waited until the doctor left the room, then looked at Zoe. "There's a large container of crab dip in the refrigerator. I made it right before I went to bed the night of the fall. If you could put some of that in a container with some crackers and bring it to me with the cookies, I'd be the happiest woman on earth."

"Aren't you worried about the nurse? I saw her on my way in. She looks like her previous employment was with the gestapo."

Sapphire waved a hand in dismissal. "Even the gestapo wouldn't dare get between me and a decent meal."

Zoe smiled. "Okay then, but you can't live on crab dip alone. What else do you want?"

"Oh, anything else is fine. My kitchen is all torn up but you were never one to cook anyway. Just pick me up stuff from the locals. With it being Cranberry Festival month, everyone will have out their best wares. It's a fine time for eating out in Everlasting."

Zoe held in a groan. She'd completely forgotten about the festival. It was an annual event that brought a flood of tourists to the small town and a bunch more local kooks out of the woodwork. Most people, her somewhat reclusive aunt included, seemed to love the festival. But Zoe viewed it as a time with crowded stores with rude patrons, people walking in the streets rather than on the sidewalks, and never being able to find a parking space near downtown.

Still, she could endure a couple of days of the aggravation for Sapphire. There were all kinds of things Zoe would endure for her aunt that she would never tolerate only for herself. And at least it looked like once her aunt was released from the hospital, she wouldn't need live-in care.

"Okay," Zoe said. "I will get you something hot for lunch and something cold for dinner. Otherwise, I'll spend more time traversing downtown than I do sitting here with you. For breakfast, do you want scones? Muffins? I can bring protein shakes, too."

"Anything is better than that. I'd rather eat this gown. Speaking of which, a change of real clothes wouldn't be so bad. And will you also bring me my Kindle from the nightstand in my bedroom? I don't expect you to sit here all day, and I don't sleep half the night."

"I came here to take care of you."

"Taking care of my cats and my home is taking care of me. Besides, you're making sure I don't starve. I'm not saying I don't want your company, but I'm not selfish enough to coop you up in a hospital all day on an uncomfortable chair, listening to the ramblings or snoring of an old woman."

"You don't ramble." It was true that sometimes a lot of what Sapphire said was "out there" as far as regular people believed, but she never rambled. She definitely snored.

Sapphire waved a hand in dismissal. "You're just being nice. Speaking of rambling, has Cornelius shown himself yet?"

"I'm not sure," Zoe said. "Is he the Maine coon with the green eyes?" That was one of Sapphire's cats that Zoe hadn't recognized.

"Cornelius isn't a cat. He's a ghost."

ZOE'S CONVERSATION with her aunt ran through her mind a million times on the way back to the lighthouse. A ghost. That declaration from her aunt was hardly the oddest thing Sapphire had ever said, and normally Zoe would have smiled and nodded and then immediately dismissed it as more of Sapphire's woo-woo stuff. The problem was that her aunt's description of Cornelius the Talkative Ghost exactly matched the man Zoe had seen that morning going down the stairs.

Zoe had been ready to dismiss the sighting as a hallucination or even a waking dream, but Sapphire had thrown a huge monkey wrench into that plan. Now Zoe was left with accepting that the lighthouse was haunted by a half-clothed ghost or that her aunt had developed the ability to make Zoe see things that weren't there.

She wasn't sure which was worse.

But none of that mattered right now. What mattered now was getting food, real clothes, and the Kindle back to Sapphire and making sure she was as comfortable as one could manage in a hospital. When she'd left that morning, Zoe had hoped she wouldn't be returning to the lighthouse until after Dane had called it quits for the day, but now she could see the folly of that thought. Sapphire was right. She couldn't sit around the hospital all day. Her aunt needed to rest, and Zoe brooding in a chair next to Sapphire's bed wouldn't be restful for either of them.

Her options now were to spend part of the time downtown in the midst of festival craziness or locked up in the lighthouse with the man she'd never gotten over. At least the lighthouse had rooms with doors and locks. She could always feign needing to lie down or work that needed addressing or an overwhelming desire to knit. Well, maybe the knitting was taking it a little too far, but common sense dictated that Dane was there to work and he wouldn't have the time or inclination to butt into her business. She could just go about regular things and he could finish up her aunt's kitchen.

His truck was still parked out front and she pulled beside it. She retrieved her suitcase from the trunk, not about to spend another morning rummaging for clean clothes, and headed inside with it. Dane was measuring a spot on the floor and looked up when she walked in.

"How is Sapphire?" he asked. "Did you see the doctor?"

Zoe nodded and repeated the doctor's prognosis to Dane.

"That's a relief," he said. "I was really worried. Sapphire's in good shape for her age, but a fall like that could hurt anyone." He looked down and spied the suitcase. "Let me take that up for you."

"That's okay. It's not that heavy and I don't want to interrupt your work. That tile is beautiful. Sapphire is going to be so happy with her new kitchen."

"I hope so."

He stared at her for a couple of very uncomfortable seconds, and she could tell he wanted to tell her something but wasn't sure how to say it. The last time she'd seen that look, he'd dumped her, which made her completely uninterested in whatever conversation he thought he wanted to have right now.

"Well, I've got to run," she said. "I have to gather up some things for Sapphire and get back to the hospital."

She started across the living room for the stairs, and he stepped out of the kitchen and in front of her.

"Wait," he said. "There's something I have to show you."

He moved past her to the coffee table and picked up a penlight and can of Mace. "What you said about Sapphire not going downstairs in her nightclothes bothered me. I forgot to tell you that when I arrived the lights were all off. There was no storm, so power shouldn't have been an issue. I couldn't figure out why the lights weren't on."

He moved to the bottom of the stairs. "I found her laid out here like this, with her arms out above her head, like she was trying to get her balance. I thought if she was holding a flashlight, she would have dropped it when it fell."

Suddenly, Zoe understood what Dane was trying to tell her. "Sapphire was carrying the penlight and Mace. The floor is uneven. They rolled under the couch, right?"

He nodded. "That's where I found them."

"Oh my God." Zoe covered her mouth with her hands. "I knew something was wrong."

"But what?"

"Something serious enough that she came down here with Mace. You said you called the sheriff's department?"

"Yeah, for what it's worth. Sheriff Bull sent September over. I requested February, but she's been partial to September lately so he gets priority when it comes to the work."

Zoe stared. "What kind of names are September and February? Have I missed some newfangled Everlasting tradition?"

Dane sighed. "Worse. Sheriff Bull is having what the local women are calling a midlife crisis. She's decided the focus of her crisis is surrounding herself with young, muscular men. She acquired so many that she decided to do a calendar of them as a fund-raiser. Since they're all from other cities, and we figure this phase will pass, we've decided it's easier to refer to them by month rather than learn all their names."

"I think I'm going to have a crisis just from listening to that. Do any of those calendar boys have law enforcement training?"

Dane shrugged. "I asked for the one I thought seemed the most intelligent, but since I've only spent a handful of seconds talking to maybe five or six of them, it's not much to go on."

"Good God. Okay, I'm going to call the sheriff and ask for...February?"

Dane nodded. "Just so you know, I took a look around earlier. All the window locks are in working condition and locked position. I'm going to make a trip to the hardware store this afternoon and change out the door locks, unless you have an objection."

Relief and appreciation coursed through Zoe. "Thank you. That makes me feel much better, especially being here alone. Sapphire has always been too loose with handing out keys to everyone. I tried to tell her, but you know how she is."

"She trusts and likes everyone."

"She doesn't like everyone, but she *is* too trusting. I really appreciate you doing this. Let me know the cost of the locks so I can repay you."

"No way. I want to do this. I don't want you scared when you're here to focus on taking care of Sapphire, and I don't want Sapphire leaving that hospital and afraid in her own home."

Zoe's jaw clenched. "I'm not going to let that happen."

THE DEPUTY who stepped out of the car looked every bit the part of a calendar model. He flashed Zoe a hundred-watt smile and strode toward her, his clingy and probably one-size-too-small uniform displaying every inch of his ripped body.

"You must be Ms. Parker," he said, and stuck out his hand. "I'm February."

Zoe glanced back at Dane, who had covered his mouth with his hand to block the smile.

"You refer to yourself as February?" she asked. "You don't find this entire calendar thing demeaning?"

"No way!" he said. "I find it flattering. Besides, my mom named me Clifford. February is a huge step up."

"All right," Zoe said, "Would you like to come inside?"

"If you don't mind," February said, "I'd rather stay out here. I've been cooped up in that office with a bunch of people all day."

"Fine, then let's get down to business," Zoe said. "You are aware of the situation with my aunt Esmerelda, correct?"

The deputy frowned. "Is that Ms. Sapphire? If so, then I'm aware that she fell down her stairs and is currently in the hospital. Sheriff Bull informed me that September processed the scene but didn't find anything to indicate a crime had occurred. Have you found something that negates his assessment?"

Zoe blinked. Of all the things she'd expected after her introduction to a man who preferred to be referred to as a month of the year, the last thing was literacy and the second to last was the possibility of competence. Maybe Dane had called this one correctly.

Feeling somewhat better about the prospects of help from law enforcement, Zoe launched into her explanation beginning with the mystery of the nightclothes and ending with Dane's find.

"So I feel that someone was in my aunt's house," Zoe said. "And that's why she went downstairs in her nightclothes. What I can't be certain of, unless she remembers, is if she tripped or if she was helped."

February looked momentarily taken aback. "I don't think someone would have pushed Ms. Parker down the stairs."

Working for a news station had left Zoe less optimistic about human nature than Deputy February. She tried again. "But you agree that my aunt went downstairs to investigate, and she must have suspected or even known that it was a person or people or she wouldn't have carried Mace with her."

February nodded. "It appears that Ms. Parker was afraid someone might be in her house, but if she knew for certain, why wouldn't she call the sheriff's department?"

"Have you met my aunt?" Zoe asked. "Spent

more than five minutes around her? She's the most stubborn individual in the world."

"Second most," Dane said, and coughed.

Zoe glared at him, then looked back at February. "She's lived alone in the lighthouse more years than I've been on this earth. The mere suggestion that she could be intimidated in her own home would be enough to prevent her from calling the cops."

"She's right," Dane agreed. "Sapphire puts a whole new spin on independence."

"So in running with the assumption that someone was in her house," Zoe continued, "what I don't know is why. She has nothing of value any more than the average person, and the lighthouse is a little out of the way to come steal a television or a DVD player."

"So what do you think they were after?" February asked, erasing all of Zoe's previous hope that law enforcement might be able to help.

Zoe threw her hands in the air. "How would I know? That's why I called you. Have there been problems with robberies? A ring of cat thieves operating in the area? Anything at all that you can suggest that explains why my aunt is in the hospital?"

February shook his head. "There hasn't been any home theft at all in the last year that I can recall. Just petty stuff from stores. Mostly kids. And I'm pretty sure there aren't any cat thieving rings."

His eyes widened. "Hey, I bet it was tourists. You know, because of the festival."

"You think tourists entered my aunt's house in the middle of the night?" Zoe asked. "Even if they managed to acquire a key, why in the world would tourists do that?"

"Because of its reputation," February said. "Everyone knows that this place is magical. People say if you make a wish and plant a penny here, your wish will be granted."

Zoe barely managed to hold in a groan. Despite being an outsider, February had been corrupted by the local myths and legends.

"And if my aunt had reported strangers on her lawn with shovels and a handful of pennies," Zoe said, "we wouldn't be having this conversation. That still wouldn't explain why someone was *inside* her house."

"Maybe they figured the magic was stronger there," February said, his completely straight face erasing any hope Zoe had that he was joking.

She decided to try another tactic. "Doesn't that sound a little dangerous to you? Especially if we go with your tourist theory? I mean, what if my aunt had gone downstairs with a nine-millimeter and opened fire? That's a big risk to take just to leave a penny on the kitchen counter."

February looked slightly horrified. "This is Maine, not LA. In LA you probably have toddlers with concealed carry licenses, but that sort of thing doesn't happen here in Everlasting."

"Actually," Zoe said, her patience completely spent, "licensing for toddlers only occurs in places like Texas. In LA they give them a stolen pistol before they put them on the street corner to deal meth."

Dane started choking and turned the opposite direction. "Sorry," he said, and held up his hand. "Swallowed a bug."

"You should get some water," February said, then turned back to face Zoe. "Look, Ms. Parker, I can appreciate what you're saying. Maybe your aunt heard someone inside her house, but we didn't find any evidence of such. Unless her memory returns and she can verify someone was inside the house, I don't think there's anything else we can do."

"Neither do I," Zoe said, in complete agreement that there was absolutely nothing local law enforcement could do if this was indeed the best of the batch. "Thank you for your time, Deputy."

"Let me know if you come up with anything solid," February said. "And I'll revisit this whole thing."

"That would be splendid," Zoe said. "Now, if you'll excuse me, there's an oven I need to go stick my head inside."

"You should tell your aunt to upgrade to one of

those self-cleaning ones," February said. "They're a lot easier."

He waved goodbye to Dane, jumped in his car, and left.

Zoe looked over at Dane, who had collapsed against the side of his truck, no longer bothering to hold in his laughter.

"Not one word," she said.

Chapter Four

Zoe headed into the hospital, loaded down with bags and frustration. The bags all contained items for her aunt. The frustration was because of her aunt. How many times had she told Sapphire not to hand out keys to her home like Halloween candy? But Zoe knew that at some point in time, probably half of Everlasting had possession of a key to her place. Making the whole "no sign of forced entry" a moot point. And despite what Deputy Pecs wanted to believe, Zoe didn't think for one moment that tourists had acquired a key to her aunt's house and entered in the middle of the night to leave pennies for magical wish-granting. In fact, that might be the most ridiculous thing she'd ever heard, and having grown up in Everlasting, that was saying a lot.

As she entered Sapphire's room, her aunt looked

up with a smile that quickly dissipated as she took in Zoe's haggard appearance.

"Why is your hair all wet?" Sapphire asked. "There wasn't a report of a storm on the news."

"That's because according to Everlasting's incredibly observant weatherman, there are no storms currently in the area. Yet standing right in your front yard, I got caught in a veritable downpour. I was soaked before I could get into the house, and the instant I stepped inside, it quit. I took time to change, but didn't bother with my hair."

"That's odd," Sapphire said. "Was anything unusual happening at the time?"

"You mean like thunder or lightning or a collection of dark clouds or a weather report that held any indication of rain? No."

"Why were you standing outside?"

"Because I'd just finished talking to the utterly and completely useless Deputy February."

Sapphire straightened in her bed. "Why was the deputy at my house? Is everything all right?"

Zoe sat the bags on the floor and took a seat in the chair next to the hospital bed. "No. Everything is definitely not all right. I was worried about you being found in your nightclothes and mentioned it to Dane. He went poking around and found something."

She went on to tell her aunt about Dane's

discovery and her useless conversation with local law enforcement.

"Does any of that spur your memory?" Zoe asked.

Sapphire, who'd been frowning during Zoe's entire delivery, slowly shook her head. "I'm sorry, but it doesn't. It's like someone cut out everything from my memory from the time I went to bed until the time I woke up here."

"But if you went downstairs in your night-clothes, with a flashlight and Mace, you thought someone was in your house, right?"

"I can't think of any other reason why I would do such a thing."

"Have you had any problems lately? Tres-passers? Anyone new in town who's taken an interest in you or the lighthouse?"

"People have always taken an interest in the lighthouse. Everyone hopes that by stepping on hallowed ground, they'll take some of the magic away with them. I keep picking pennies out of my herb garden."

Zoe held in a sigh. She'd heard the legend of the lighthouse a million times. One of her ancestors had commissioned its construction because they'd lost too many fishermen due to mostly submerged rocks just off the coast. Coming in at night, they sometimes missed the narrow channel that allowed them proper passage. One day, three large fishing boats got caught out in a storm and couldn't get back to port before dark. They approached the coast at what they thought was the correct entry point, but were headed straight for the rocks. Suddenly, the lighthouse beacon came on and illuminated the waters. A tiny tip of one of the rocks glittered in the light and the ships corrected their path before crashing onto them. When the fishermen went to the lighthouse to thank whoever it was that had fired up the beacon at just the right moment, they were shocked to find the structure empty and the beacon sitting on the floor on the bottom level, not yet installed.

Decades ago, large channel markers were installed, providing safe passage for the fishermen, so the lighthouse had been decommissioned and the city had accepted Sapphire's bid for its purchase. But the legend had remained a core part of Everlasting history and was included in every book, magazine, or article about the town. Which meant that if magic wishes were really at the bottom of the break-in, then that limited the number of suspects to everyone who'd ever crossed the county line.

Well, she could probably eliminate two people— herself and Dane. She had been on the opposite coast and Dane had access all day. No reason to sneak in during the middle of the night when you had been invited in through the front door.

"Has there been anything lately that was out of

the ordinary compared to the norm?" Zoe asked, trying another tactic. "Anyone a repeat? Anyone ask to come inside? Anyone get pushy or too nosy for your liking?"

Sapphire scrunched her brow in concentration. "The cats!" she finally said. "They've been odd lately. Prowling around more than usual, knocking things off tables. I thought it was Cornelius causing it, but he's usually in another room when they do it. I've discussed respect for my property with them several times in the last couple weeks, but they are ignoring me. I have yet to figure out why."

When Sapphire said she had discussed respect with the cats, Zoe knew she really meant it. As in, gathered them all in one room and had a mini board meeting. Zoe would be the first to admit that her aunt's cats were trained better than she'd ever thought cats could be. Sapphire was convinced she could talk to them and that they understood everything she said. If only that were true and the cats could talk back, then maybe they could find out what had them spooked. Because that's exactly what their behavior sounded like.

"What about predators?" Zoe asked. "Bear, coyotes, skunk? Anything lurking around outside that could be bothering them?"

"Those things are in the woods, sometimes closer than others, but the cats have never been bothered by wildlife before."

Okay. Nothing there, so time for another train of thought. "Do you have anything of value that someone might want to steal? Something outside of regular household stuff?"

Sapphire shook her head. "I'm afraid I sold off all my diamonds to purchase my castle in France."

"You would have purchased a cat farm in Florida."

Sapphire smiled. "You know me too well. But I can't think of anything worth breaking in for. All of my furniture is older but not old enough to be antique. Even the stuff that meets the criteria isn't from a period or a craftsman that makes it worth risking prison over. The only thing of value, and that's probably only to me, are the journals my ancestors kept."

Sapphire's great-grandfather was a fisherman and one of the founding members of Everlasting. He had kept journals of his travels and of the building of the town. He was the one who'd commissioned the construction of the lighthouse. Several of Sapphire's other ancient relatives had followed the same practice of recording their daily lives. Offhand, Zoe couldn't think of any reason for someone to be interested in the journals, but she'd take a look at them tonight. It wasn't as if she had anything else to go on.

Sapphire looked so concerned that Zoe reached

up and squeezed her arm. "Don't worry about it. We're going to figure this out."

"You have a life all the way across the country that you have to get back to."

"I'm not leaving here until I'm sure you're safe."

Even if it meant the job she'd sacrificed the last six years for was at risk.

DANE WAS STORING his saws in the shed when she pulled up. He put the shiny new padlock in place and headed her direction.

"I got both door locks replaced," he said. "Figured it wouldn't hurt to replace the padlock too."

Zoe nodded. "I really appreciate you doing this. I'm not sure I could have changed out the hardware myself, and calling someone else to do it sorta defeats the purpose when we don't know who the bad guy is."

"You're smart to be cautious. I don't want to think that someone I know could be responsible for this, but it's stupid to rule someone out just because you think you know them. Did you tell Sapphire what we found? Has she remembered anything?"

Zoe's shoulders slumped. The length of the day and the ground covered had finally caught up with her, and now she was about to do something she knew she shouldn't do. "Can I tell you over something with alcohol in it? I'm beat."

"You do look exhausted, and I have never turned down an offer of alcohol."

They headed inside and Dane pointed to the living room. "Go sit down. I'll grab the drinks."

She knew she should argue. After all, she was the host, so to speak, but being overwhelmed with too much useless information and not enough relevant data was taxing her already tired body and mind. She trudged into the living room and sank into her aunt's recliner, then after a second of thought, grabbed the remote and lifted the leg rest. No sense in relaxing halfway.

Dane came into the living room with a glass of wine for her and a beer for him and smiled when he saw her kicked back in the chair. "You weren't lying about wanting to sit down."

She took a sip of the wine and sighed. "This has been one of the longest and most frustrating days of my life."

"I take it Sapphire wasn't any help?" he asked as he sat on the couch.

Zoe shook her head. "She still can't remember and even if she could, unless she could identify whoever was here, what difference would it make?"

"I guess we'd know for certain that someone was in the lighthouse. We're operating off that assumption given the evidence, but we can't be sure that was the case."

"Well, until I know different, I'm going to proceed as if there were an intruder. And since we don't appear to have an easy way to figure out who it was, the next best thing is to figure out why they were here."

"Makes sense."

"It does, right? Except I asked Sapphire about valuables…anything that would be worth risking jail time to steal, but she can't think of anything. There's no family jewels, no secret Monets hidden in a closet somewhere. She has her money down at the credit union, not tucked away in a cool wall safe hidden behind a secret panel."

Dane smiled. "It sounds like you've covered all the bases. So what do we do now?"

She knew it shouldn't bother her, but his reference to "we" sent her right back to the past where the word meant something. Meant they were a couple. Suddenly, it felt as though the room were closing in on her and all she could see was Dane, getting closer and closer, taking up more space. This had been a mistake. She couldn't "hang out" casually with the man she'd never lost feelings for, even if she hadn't been aware of those unlost feelings until she'd set foot back in Everlasting.

"There's nothing we can do, at least not at the moment," she said. "I'm too tired to think and you've got to go home to eat, shower, rest, and do whatever else it is you do when you're not working."

He nodded and rose, sensing her dismissal. "Are you sure you're all right staying here alone?"

"With you changing the locks, I'm safer tonight than last night."

He pulled keys out of his pocket and handed them to her. "The larger two open the front and back door. The small key is for the padlock on the shed. I kept a set for myself...at least until I finish up the work. I hope that's all right."

"Of course."

He took a card out of his wallet and handed it to her. "That's my personal cell phone number. If you hear anything tonight or think of anything else I can do, call me."

She took the card and sighed. "I'm guessing you're a better bet than local law enforcement. If they bothered to show up, they'd probably come with a handful of pennies."

"Oh, I'm sure they'd come out. But even driving at a decent clip, the lighthouse is at least ten minutes from town." He grinned. "And the handful of pennies would probably slow him down even more because he'd be clutching them while he drove."

"Promise me you have a better weapon than ripped abs."

"I hunt, remember? And I bought the property

just down the coast. I can be here armed and in appropriate clothing in a matter of minutes."

"You bought the old Miller place? The last time I saw it, one entire side had collapsed in."

He nodded. "It looks a little different now. Well, completely different, actually. What I really paid for was the land. I bulldozed the old house and built a new one. It's small but perfect for me. It's all about the view, right?"

"That's what they say."

"Maybe you can see it before you leave."

Her body flushed at the thought of being alone with Dane in his house. "Maybe so," she managed.

"I'll lock up on my way out and turn on the front light. The weather report has changed again. No storms in the forecast tonight, so you should be okay as far as power is concerned. But if it goes out, call me. Until we figure out what's going on here, I don't want you sitting around in the dark, and I don't want you going outside in the middle of the night alone to fire up the generator."

She hadn't thought about the power outage since last night and wasn't happy to be reminded about her fickle power source. All she could do was pray that the fall storms that seemed to blow in from the Atlantic every other day would give her a break until all this was sorted out and Sapphire was safely back in her home.

"If I lose power and I'm awake to notice, I'll call," she said.

"Good enough. Then I'll see you tomorrow. Same time."

She nodded and he headed out of the house, locking the door behind him. Zoe downed the rest of her wine and pushed herself out of the recliner. As tired as she was, she had things to do before going to bed. First, a long, hot shower. Then she was going to start going through everything in the lighthouse.

Something inside had captured an intruder's attention.

And she was going to figure out what it was.

DANE GLANCED in his rearview mirror as he pulled away from the lighthouse. He didn't want to leave but couldn't see that he had much choice in the matter. He couldn't work all night, and Zoe would never agree to letting him stay even if she thought there was a credible threat to her safety. The reality was, Dane couldn't be certain there wasn't. Granted, she'd been all right the night before, but if word had gotten around that Sapphire was in the hospital, whoever had entered her house before might think it was a golden opportunity to try again, especially if he was unaware that Zoe was in residence.

Still, his options were limited. The driveway to the lighthouse was narrow and could be easily seen from any of the windows facing it, so no sitting in his truck to keep watch. Short of lurking in the woods and fighting the mosquitoes all night, his only other option was to go home and hope she called if anything went south.

Or…a thought occurred to him.

He could head to the Magic Eight Ball and see if there was any local gossip about Sapphire or maybe other residents reporting prowlers. Plus, several of the old-timers were there drinking their retirement away every night. He could always tax their whiskey-laden memories and see if any of them knew of a reason someone would risk a go at the lighthouse.

He turned his truck toward Main Street and cursed when he saw the line of cars circling like sharks for a parking space. The Cranberry Festival always brought a lot of people to Everlasting, but this year the tiny town seemed to be overflowing with cars and people and strollers and dogs. To those who preferred the normally quiet downtown area with its quaint shops and quirky owners, it was like an invasion of suburbia.

He turned onto a side street and found a parking space. It would be easier and quicker to walk than to drive around in circles with everyone else. Logically, he knew that the festival brought much-needed cash flow into the town, but irrationally, he wished Everlasting would hit some sort of town lottery and cancel the entire thing.

The Magic Eight Ball was a pool hall and bar that had been located at the end of Main Street since there had been a Main Street. Rumor had it that it had gone up right after the town hall and the church. At least Everlasting had its priorities straight. And the best part about the pool hall was that it wasn't on the list of hot spots for festival attendees. The couples without children preferred the newer trendy bars located on the waterfront.

The bar was filled with all the regulars, most of whom Dane had known his entire life. He made his way through the crowd, giving out an occasional hello or wave, and finally stepped up to the bar. Shorty, the owner and chief bartender, gave him a nod and pushed his usual beer across the counter.

"Surprised to see you in here tonight," Shorty said.

"Why is that?" Dane had spent more than a few nights in the bar shooting the breeze with the owner and the old fishermen.

"Heard your girlfriend was back in town. Thought you might have business elsewhere."

"Zoe hasn't been my girlfriend for a very long

time. The only reason I have 'business' with her is because she's here to check on her aunt."

Shorty let out a guffaw. "Don't get your back all up. I was just giving you some grief. I heard about Sapphire. How's she doing?"

"She's going to be all right, but they're keeping her in the hospital a few more days. Concussion."

"Sapphire was already crazy. How are they supposed to figure out when she's better?"

"X-rays, I suppose."

Shorty nodded. "Guess that works. Tell Zoe I'd love to say hello if she has the time."

"Will do." Dane grabbed his beer and scanned the back of the bar and spotted two of the old fishermen he was looking for. He headed over, and they smiled when they saw him and pulled a chair up to their table.

"I see you braved the festival crowd," Monte Gallagher said. "A bit of a trial to get a beer around here the month of October."

"What the hell are you talking about?" Sam Chester said. "You live right behind the bar."

"Still gotta dodge 'em on the sidewalk," Monte said.

All three of them laughed.

"I heard you're doing work out at Sapphire's place," Monte said. "She got you building houses for all those cats?"

"No," Dane said. "She's remodeling the lighthouse—bringing the kitchen and the bathrooms up to date."

Monte huffed. "Had the same bathroom since 1963. Still works fine."

"Ha. Tell that to the grout in your tub that retired in the '80s," Sam said. "One night, that tub is going to fall clean through the floor with you in it. They're going to have to haul you off to the hospital naked as a jaybird."

Dane grimaced. "I can take a look at that for you when I'm done with Sapphire's place."

"I guess it wouldn't hurt to have you take a look," Monte said, "but I'm not doing no expensive renovation. If the water runs and the toilet flushes, then that's all people need to be doing in a bathroom anyway."

Sam rolled his eyes and looked over at Dane. "My niece works at the hospital. She said Sapphire had a fall and is taking a couple days of vacation with them. Concussion, my niece says."

Dane nodded. "The doctor said she's going to be all right, but that's why I came in tonight. I was hoping to ask you guys something."

"If it's doctoring advice you're after," Monte said, "my cure for everything is right there in that glass." He pointed to his whiskey.

"I'll leave the doctoring advice to the doctors. This is more personal. Zoe is in town to see to her aunt, and she thinks someone broke into Sapphire's house and that's why she fell...coming down the stairs in the dark to see what was going on."

"What the hell is the girl talking about?" Monte asked. "Sapphire's older than Sam here, and his first fishing trip was when Moses parted the Red Sea."

"Unfortunately, there's good reason for Zoe to think that," Dane said and explained about the nightclothes and finding the penlight and the Mace. "The problem is, Sapphire can't remember and there's no guarantee she ever will. And even if she could remember that she heard someone in her house, it still doesn't mean she'd know why they were there."

"And you think we'd know?" Sam said. "You sure you weren't hitting the whiskey before you walked in here? We don't know anything about thieving. The only crime we're involved in is drinking too much and maybe a little commenting on women, but that's not illegal. At least most times it's not."

"You might not know about thieving but you do know all the local gossip," Dane said.

"That's probably true enough," Monte said. "So what kind of gossip are you looking for?"

"Sapphire doesn't really have anything of value," Dane said. "At least, not something worth driving out all that way and risking jail over. But with the Cranberry Festival going on, I got to thinking that maybe there was some legend about the lighthouse…like buried treasure. Something worth the risk to break into her house."

"Buried treasure, huh?" Monte mused. "Plenty of those tales in these parts, but I can't say as I've heard any specific to the lighthouse."

Sam frowned. "What about the magic stone?"

Monte's eyes widened. "I haven't heard that yarn since I was a boy. Even if someone still remembered that story, surely they wouldn't take it as the gospel."

Sam shrugged. "A fool is born every minute."

"These days, more than one," Monte said.

"So is anyone going to tell me the story?" Dane asked.

"Don't see what it could hurt," Sam said. "The stone was said to come from Wales from the time of King Arthur. It had been touched by Merlin himself and had magical properties. It disappeared for over a thousand years, then was rumored to have been found and smuggled out of England by a group of colonists who thought the stone would bring them good fortune in America."

Monte nodded. "But the colonists' ship was attacked by pirates and the stone disappeared along with a chest of gold coins. You know those coins as the Princess Gold."

Dane stared. "But those were found here decades ago. Some of them are in a museum in Portland."

"But the stone was never found," Sam said. "The legend says one of the colonists hid it in his pocket. The pirates threw them off the ship, but despite a raging storm, they made it to shore."

"Because the magic of the stone protected them," Monte said.

"So what happened to them after that?" Dane asked.

"The legend says they settled in what would eventually become Everlasting. That they buried the stone somewhere and that's what brought the original magic to this area."

"What did the stone look like?"

"Green," Monte said, "and the size of a walnut."

"An emerald," Dane said. "I guess that fits. Emeralds offer protection at sea and are the stones of rebirth."

Monte raised one eyebrow at him.

"What?" Dane asked. "You think I've lived here my entire life and haven't picked up on some things? Doesn't mean I buy into it, but I can respect that other people do."

Sam nodded. "That's what I always say. All the fanciful tales aren't hurting anyone. In fact, they probably keep a bit of the town's money supply flowing."

"Probably," Dane said. "So how come I've never heard this story?"

"I don't think I've ever known but a handful of people who knew it," Sam said. "My grandmother told it to me, but my mother wasn't a believer in such things, so the story passed along when my grandmother did. I imagine that's the way it was with most families."

Monte nodded. "People can easily believe in buried gold coins because they've been found and the pillaging of pirates is documented, but who's going to swear to the existence of a magic stone touched by a man that most say never existed?"

Dane frowned. "I don't know."

But he wondered.

Chapter Five

Zoe stepped out of the shower and grabbed a thick white towel to dry off. It felt like Kleenex against her skin and she made a mental note to ask Sapphire where she'd gotten them. Zoe wasn't one to spend a lot of money on luxury items, but these towels would be worth a dip in her bank account.

She combed through her hair and left it hanging loose to dry. It was the one advantage to having board-straight hair—no styling required. No matter what she did to it, her hair always looked the same with ten minutes of gravity working on it. One less thing to hassle with. She pulled on her turquoise-and-pink pajamas, stuck her feet in her fuzzy pink slippers, and headed down to the kitchen to see about dinner.

She'd picked up an extra sandwich when she'd made the food run for Sapphire. Right now, the roast beef sandwich and sea-salt-and-cracked-pepper chips she'd snagged sounded as good as filet mignon and scalloped potatoes. She'd skipped breakfast entirely and had picked at a salad for lunch while Sapphire ate clam chowder. Hunger hadn't even entered Zoe's thoughts earlier, but now she was starving.

She grabbed the sandwich, the chips, and a diet soda and flopped into the recliner, deciding it had been surprisingly comfortable earlier. The television remote was on a table next to the chair, so she turned on the TV and kicked back to watch some of those complainers on HGTV and eat her dinner. She'd just finished her sandwich and yelling at a couple who wanted an updated mansion for a budget of a hundred thousand when her cell phone rang. She grabbed her phone off the end table and was surprised to see Dane's name in the display.

"Hello?"

"I hope I didn't wake you," he said.

"It's only eight o'clock. I'm a good forty years away from going to bed this early."

He laughed. "Fair enough, but you were exhausted earlier and I figure you didn't sleep well after traveling, so I thought you might have called it quits sooner than usual."

The thought had definitely crossed her mind, but now that she'd had a shower and food, she felt a hundred percent better. "I still might turn in early," she said, "but not quite yet. Is something wrong?"

"No. But there was something I wanted to share with you."

He told her about his stopping by the Magic Eight Ball and his conversation with Monte and Sam. "Have you ever heard that story?"

"I don't think so, and I thought I'd heard them all."

"It probably doesn't mean anything," he said. "But I thought I'd tell you so that you could ask Sapphire about it. I figure if anyone knows about a magic emerald buried somewhere in Everlasting, it would be her."

"I guess treasure seekers looking for a stone that likely never existed is as good a possibility as any. And one I could live with a lot better than someone breaking into Sapphire's home just to hurt her."

"If that's the case, then whoever did it better hope Deputy February catches them before I do."

A flood of warmth washed over Zoe. Sapphire might not have any blood relatives left in Everlasting, but it was nice to know people cared so much about her. Despite everything that had happened between them, Dane was a good guy. It was just a shame that there were so many differences in what they wanted out of life. And not the negotiable, meet-in-the-middle kind of differences. In order for them to have stayed together, one of them would have had to abandon everything important to them. Neither had been willing to do that.

"I really appreciate everything you're doing," Zoe said.

"No way am I letting you deal with this alone. I'm going to hop in the shower myself. Try to get some rest."

Zoe said goodbye and blew out a breath. Great. Now she was imagining Dane in the shower. The image was nice but not remotely restful. She hopped out of the recliner and headed through the makeshift kitchen and into the laundry room... where the firing squad awaited.

All ten cats were lined up, glaring at her, their empty food bowls behind them.

"Crap!" Zoe tossed out her sandwich wrapper and opened the cabinet. The cats had all been camped out in their selected spot of sunlight when she'd gone upstairs earlier, but apparently, the dinner bell had rung and she'd missed the cue.

The cans of cat food were stacked by flavor with a label on the shelf that indicated which cat the meal belonged to. Ten cats. Six different flavors. That was a lot to keep straight. No wonder Sapphire had labels, and thank goodness for it. When Zoe left home, all her aunt's cats had eaten the same dry food. Apparently, everyone had gotten an attitude and a subsequent dietary upgrade. Or maybe Sapphire had decided the fancy food was deserved because of the whole toilet thing.

She opened the cans and dumped the food into the individually marked bowls, then stood back, waiting for the cat fight she figured was coming. Amazingly, each cat went to its own bowl and started eating without incident. Zoe had never really believed her aunt could actually communicate with animals, but she'd be the first to admit that Sapphire definitely had a way with them. One of her coworkers in LA had one cat and went through a set of mini-blinds every other week.

But as far as Zoe was concerned, the most impressive thing Sapphire had accomplished was no litter boxes. It sometimes meant the bathroom you rushed to might be in use, and Zoe knew firsthand you definitely didn't pop into one in the middle of the night without turning on a light, but it was a small price to pay for no litter scooping. If Sapphire could teach other people how to do it, she'd make a mint.

With her culinary responsibilities wrapped up for the night and a new burst of energy coursing through her, Zoe decided to forgo the early bedtime and instead head up to her aunt's bedroom and go through the journals. Zoe didn't believe for a minute that a magical emerald was somewhere on the property, but it was entirely possible that someone thought hidden treasure could be contained in the lighthouse, or that Sapphire had information on said treasure in the old documents she'd kept. Her aunt had never made a secret about the journals' existence. In fact, she'd talk about the old legends and tales to anyone who would listen.

Zoe made a mental note to ask her aunt if she'd told those stories to anyone new lately, but was afraid with the festival going on, there could be a long list of strangers who'd been inundated with tales from Sapphire in the line at the grocery store, the coffee shop, random places on the sidewalk downtown, and pretty much anywhere else Sapphire could manage a captive audience for her favorite subject.

She headed upstairs to her aunt's bedroom and was surprised to find the entire room had been redone. A light blue paint covered the previously dull brown walls, and new distressed white furniture filled the room. The headboard and footboard of the bed looked like planks from an old ship, and a matching dresser stood on the opposite wall. A row of bookcases lined the longest wall and a small desk stood right in front of the picture window that looked out over the ocean. A white quilt with blue seashells and matching pillowcases covered the bed.

Zoe sighed. It was perfect and lovely, and she was so happy her aunt had finally spent some money on herself. Sapphire was incredibly generous with local charities and the care of her cats, but always balked at spending money on her own behalf. Zoe had to admit that after all those years of pushing her own desires aside, her aunt was making up for lost time.

She crossed the room and stepped into the bathroom, expecting greatness after seeing the bedroom, and she wasn't disappointed. The same blue paint from the bedroom was carried into the bathroom. White marble tile covered the floor and made up the sides of a shower stall in the corner. But the focal point was the claw-foot tub in the center of the back wall. Zoe didn't even want to imagine what it had taken to get the tub upstairs, but no matter how much trouble it had been, it was all worth it. The entire suite was absolutely perfect.

She stepped back into the bedroom and headed over to the bookcases. The journals took up two shelves. It was going to be a long night. Zoe snagged a stack of them and headed over to the desk. At least she'd have a beautiful view while she worked.

The sun had long since disappeared, but the moon hung over the ocean like a giant spotlight, reflecting on the ripples of current. In the distance, Zoe could see the tiny lights of approaching ships and the brighter glow of the channel markers, guiding them back to port. It was so peaceful and serene and nothing like the loud, busy parking lot her studio apartment in LA looked out over.

She grabbed the first journal off the stack and

opened it up, trying to block where her thoughts had headed. Everything had a cost. And her career meant living in a large urban area. LA was a prime market, and she had a highly desirable job positioned perfectly for the career she'd always wanted. A great view would have to wait until she was so popular she could demand a high salary. Or until she won the lottery.

She shook her head and turned her attention to the journal, scanning the text for any references to jewels, coins, treasure, pirates, secrets, or hidden things. It took her an hour to review the first five journals and she'd found exactly nothing. Except an inordinate number of references to the size of the catch for the day and the number of available women in various ports along the coastline.

Her back was protesting sitting so long without movement, so she rose from the chair and stretched, deliberating heading downstairs to snag the sack of cookies she'd picked up at the coffee shop. Sapphire wasn't the only one with a weakness for cranberry cookies. As she headed for the door, she heard a noise downstairs. It was faint, but it sounded as if something had fallen onto the hardwood floor. The rug would have masked the sound, and tile produced a higher pitch when things hit it, so she surmised it came from the living room.

Chastising herself for not bringing the Mace upstairs with her, she eased over to her aunt's nightstand and opened it, praying her aunt kept a spare. She had one in her suitcase, but that was in her bedroom and there was no way to get to it quickly or to open the suitcase without making a lot of noise. She felt a bit of relief when she saw another can of Mace in the corner of the drawer and pulled it out. Her cell phone was on the desk, and she grabbed it with her left hand. Briefly, she considered calling Dane, but the last thing she wanted to do was get him over here late at night because one of the cats was strolling across tables, likely protesting Sapphire's absence or their delayed dinner.

She'd head downstairs and if the noise got worse or she decided it was more racket than cats could make, then she'd hurry back upstairs, lock herself in her aunt's room, and call Dane and the cops. It was a solid plan.

Clutching the Mace and the phone, she crept down the stairs, wincing every time the wood creaked. The lighthouse was eerily silent, which was a plus for her being able to hear someone else but also a negative for them being able to hear her. Besides, it just felt creepy. Like even the air was still.

She made it to the second-floor landing and paused to listen, but nothing stirred downstairs and not even a wisp of air could be heard outside. She drew in a deep breath and said a quick prayer. It was now or never.

She slipped around the stairwell wall and

headed down the last stretch of stairs to the first floor. This was it. Either it was nothing but a cat or she might be in for the same scenario as her aunt. Only in her case, she wasn't going to make it easy on them and fall. She was going to go out in a blaze of Mace-spraying glory.

The narrow stairwell allowed for a limited view of the rooms below. Basically, all she could see was a stretch from the bottom of the stairs and halfway to the front door. The good news was, there was no storm, and she'd left the light on downstairs. So far, so good. No noise and no sign of movement, at least from her limited viewpoint.

When she reached the last step, she paused again to steady her nerves, then with her finger on the Mace trigger, she jumped off the last step into the living room, arm in front of her and Mace ready to fire. She scanned the room, her head twisting back as forth so quickly it would probably be sore tomorrow morning, but she didn't see anything.

Frowning, she lowered her arm and walked into the center of the living room, checking the floor for anything that used to be sitting on a table. When she reached an occasional table in front of a window, she found the culprit. An old compass that usually sat on the table was on the floor directly in front of it, and the doily that covered the table was slid over to one side.

It was just one of the cats having a moment.

Zoe sighed and wondered how long it would take her heart to stop pounding so loudly that she could practically hear it. This was yet one more reason she was not getting a pet. She wasn't at home enough for one anyway, but the cats' habit of spooking for no reason and suddenly needing to be in another room was something she didn't want to deal with on a daily basis. She didn't get enough sleep as it was. The last thing she needed was a sketchy cat sprinting through her studio apartment all night, and there was enough going on in the parking lot below her unit to spook a veteran cop, much less a cat.

Since she was already downstairs, she decided to grab a soda and the cookies. As long as she wasn't sleepy, she might as well continue reviewing the journals. And that review would be a lot more pleasant with little bites of cranberry-and-vanilla goodness.

Given that her pajamas had no pockets, her hands were full as she made her way back upstairs. If this packhorsing up and down the stairs continued for more than two days, she was ordering a pink fanny pack to match her pajamas. Or maybe a backpack. That would leave her hands free for the cell phone and Mace.

Her mind focused on the cookies, she took the last few steps at a half jog and stepped into her aunt's bedroom, ready to open the bag and get down to the most important business of the night. And then she realized she wasn't alone.

The half-dressed man stood in the middle of Sapphire's bedroom, a confused expression on his face. In keeping with every B horror movie that Zoe had ever watched, she screamed and dropped everything she'd been carrying, including the phone and the Mace.

Immediately, she squatted, then panicked over which item to pick up first. Finally she settled on the Mace, figuring she'd disable him first, then call for help. She sprang up and leveled the can at him. His eyes widened and he put up a hand to protest, but she wasn't having any of it.

"Take that," she said, and pressed the trigger on the can.

The stream of liquid flew directly at the man's face and then passed right through him and arced onto the floor behind him. He turned around to look down at the liquid pooling on the floor, then turned back around to face Zoe again.

"It can't be," she said. "There's no such thing as ghosts."

"That's good to hear," the man said. "It means I'm not really dead."

Zoe stared at him, unable to blink, unable to think. This couldn't be happening. She must be imagining it.

Again?

Okay, having the same waking nightmare twice didn't seem viable, especially when her aunt had described her nightmare down to the plaid boxers, but Zoe still wasn't ready to run with the whole ghost thing. Not yet.

She reached over with her left hand and pinched her arm, narrowing her eyes at the man. Nope. He was still there. She pinched harder.

"You're going to bruise if you keep doing that," he said. "Let me make this easy on you. My name is Cornelius and I'm dead."

"No." Zoe shook her head. "You can't be real, because that would mean that witches and were-wolves and fairies might exist as well."

"What are you talking about? Fairies haven't been seen in centuries. I knew quite a few witches in my time, but not the kind that could cast a spell." He started laughing and Zoe stared, not sure whether to cry or drink. So far, drinking was winning.

She took a step toward him, then another, and when she was close enough, she leaned forward and reached out with her fingertips to touch him. She drew back her hand when it passed right through him and the air was colder.

"I don't believe it," she said. "You're real. A ghost. And real."

"You don't look so good," he said. "Maybe you

should sit down or breathe into a paper bag or something."

"Sitting will work," she said, moving over to the chair in front of the desk and sliding onto it.

She closed her eyes and drew in a deep breath, then slowly blew it out, but when she opened her eyes again, he was still standing there.

"Okay," she said finally. "I'm going to roll with this. Mainly because I don't see another option. So you're a ghost and your name is Cornelius?"

"That's me."

"Where did you come from? I've certainly never seen you before and I spent a lot of time in this lighthouse before moving away. And until last night, I've never heard my aunt mention you."

Cornelius shrugged. "I don't know where I came from. One day, I was just here."

"How long have you been here?"

"I don't know. Time doesn't really matter much when that's all you've got and there's plenty of it. But I think it was right after what Sapphire refers to as The Great Chicken Escape."

Zoe thought back to when Sapphire's friend Zelda—also not her given name—had decided that owning chickens would be a good idea and had moved them onto her back porch. One night, Zelda forgot to latch the door and the chickens had invited themselves out for a stroll. It didn't end well for several of the chickens, or Zelda, who ended up with a sprained ankle after chasing them half the night, but there was a pretty happy fox strolling around the next day. Sapphire had told her that story, barely managing to get it out between peals of laughter, right after Zoe had moved away.

"About six years?" Zoe asked.

"If you say so."

"Okay, but I still don't understand why," she said. "Ghosts are supposed to come back for a reason—at least that's how it is in the movies. You're supposed to be exacting revenge against the people who wronged you or preventing some great tragedy from occurring."

Cornelius frowned. "Six years would be a bit too much lead time on a tragedy, and I can't do anything about people who wronged me. They died years ago. That's the first thing Sapphire checked for me."

"So you just lurk around here, scaring people? Can you at least put on a full set of clothes?"

"You think I'm happy about this? This is the way I was buried and I haven't figured out how to change it yet. This coat goes with my best pair of trousers. That louse cousin of mine who poisoned me not only ran off with my wife but did it in my favorite pair of pants."

He sighed. "I really miss those pants."

"Not your wife?"

"Not really. He could have had her if he'd

asked. He didn't have to kill me for her. Maybe for the pants, though."

"So if you have no business that you have to attend to here, why don't you leave?"

"Do you think I haven't tried? I head outside and start walking but every time I get to the forest, I feel this huge rush of blood to my head and then I'm right back in the lighthouse. I can walk all the way down the path to the ocean, but if I step one foot into the water, same thing." He grinned. "But look at the upside. You always have someone around to talk to."

"Goody. I take it you don't talk to Dane?"

Surely he would have mentioned the talking ghost during any one of their discussions of strange things happening at the lighthouse.

Cornelius shook his head. "Men don't ever see or hear me. Only women."

Lucky us.

Suddenly, a thought occurred to Zoe. "Were you in the lighthouse when my aunt fell?"

"Of course. Who do you think woke her up? Darn woman sleeps like the dead—if you'll pardon the expression—especially when she takes one of those sleeping pills. I almost went hoarse yelling."

"Wait. Sapphire takes sleeping pills? Since when?"

Cornelius shrugged. "She was having trouble sleeping. Used to pace her bedroom most of the night. Couldn't sleep during the day, either. The doctor said insomnia sometimes happens with age and gave her these pills to take when she couldn't sleep."

"And she took one that night?"

"Yeah. I talked to her right before she went to bed and she had one out with a glass of water on her nightstand."

"I bet that didn't help with the memory loss thing, either." Zoe had a friend who'd been prescribed sleeping pills, and after the police discovered her wandering in the middle of the street in an evening gown—none of which she remembered—she'd decided it was better to exercise herself into exhaustion in order to get some rest.

Cornelius nodded. "I was about to start spooking the cats, hoping one of them would take a run across her and wake her up. All of them can see me but they usually dash off and hide when I'm around."

Which probably explained why one of them had taken flight off the occasional table earlier. "Why were you trying to wake Sapphire up?" she asked, a bit confused now that she had put everything he'd said into perspective.

"Because those men were in her kitchen and they didn't belong there."

Zoe felt her pulse spike. "You *saw* people in her kitchen the night she fell?"

"Of course. Two of them."

"Did you recognize them?"

He shook his head. "They were wearing ski masks."

Zoe struggled to control her disappointment. For a second, she'd thought this entire mess was going wrap itself up on the eyewitness testimony of a ghost. "Other than the masks, what did they look like?"

"Tall. One thinner. One heavier-set but not fat. The bigger must have been the leader because he did all the pointing and talking."

"What did he say?"

"He said a stone was somewhere on this property and Sapphire had a map. Then they started digging through the drawers in the coffee table and end tables. That's when I ran upstairs to get your aunt."

"And what happened after that? Did they hurt Sapphire?"

"They never touched her, but they caused her to fall. When she came downstairs, the leader shone a flashlight directly in her eyes and blinded her. She stepped wrong and fell down the last three steps or so. I ran into the laundry room where some of the cats were hiding and chased them all into the living room. All those cats zooming around freaked the men out and they left."

"They got freaked out by a bunch of cats?"

"Have you ever seen ten cats throwing a fit? It's not something you want to be in the middle of, and the beams from the flashlights zipping around the room only made it worse. The thinner one started yelling about demons and witches and bolted out the door. The leader went over and took a closer look at Sapphire, then ran after him."

"Did they leave on foot or in a car?"

"It was a truck...a dark color, but I can't be certain if it was black or blue. It was cloudy that night so there wasn't any moonlight to help." He looked worried. "I wish I could have seen more. Sapphire is a really nice lady. She agreed to let me hang out inside the lighthouse as long as I promise not to stroll around all the time stirring up the cats or walk into the bathroom when she's in there or her bedroom when she's sleeping. I broke my promise that night."

"I'm sure that time was okay with Sapphire."

"She's not mad at me? Did she say that?"

"I'm afraid not. My aunt doesn't remember anything about that night except going to bed. The next thing she remembers is waking up in the hospital. I told Dane all of this when I got back from the hospital. Didn't you hear any of it?"

He shook his head. "I was out for most of the day. I like to sit on the big stone at the end of the path and watch the ships and sailboats as they go by. I used to love sailing. Now I can't even dip a toe into the water." His expression turned wistful as he looked out the window.

"Okay." Zoe rose from the chair and started pacing. There was a lot to absorb and she was currently overflowing. She had accepted that Cornelius was real and was a ghost, although assimilating that knowledge into her daily life was going to take a bit more time. She also had confirmation that her aunt had indeed fallen because of intruders.

Oddly enough, the hardest thing to process was that two people not only believed some old legend that she didn't even remember, but they had broken into the lighthouse to steal a treasure map that probably didn't even exist. So all she had to do was figure out who else knew the legend of the magic emerald and thought that bit of fiction was worth risking prison time over. Dane could help with background on anyone Sapphire remembered.

And maybe—just to be thorough with the investigation—she'd ask her aunt about that treasure map. It couldn't possibly be true, but as long as she was going to play Scooby-Doo with Cornelius the Chatty Ghost, then she might as well do it right. She looked over at Cornelius, who was watching her pace, and flopped back down in the chair again.

Now all she had to figure out was how to explain all of this to Dane without him wrapping her up in a straitjacket.

HE WATCHED the lighthouse from the nearby woods. Lights were on downstairs and up on the third floor. The blinds were closed, but he could see slivers of light peeking out through the cracks. Not only was the lighthouse inhabited, it had apparently been taken over by a night owl. His options weren't any better in the daytime, either. The contractor was there every day and usually didn't leave for lunch. He'd hoped the lighthouse would be empty for several nights with the old woman in the hospital, but a younger replacement had shown up before he could get back inside. He'd been working the night before and hadn't had the opportunity to come back to the lighthouse, but given that the other woman had already taken up residence, it wouldn't have done him any good anyway.

He'd watched the contractor this afternoon when he changed the locks. It was inconvenient that his key would no longer work, but not a huge problem. Nothing the contractor had bought in the Everlasting hardware store would be overly difficult to bypass.

If only his partner hadn't freaked over those damned cats.

Okay, so he'd admit that he thought it was creepy...all he could see in the bursts of his flashlight was fur and claws and teeth. And the sound.

Who knew cats could sound that scary? Granted, at that point, the cats weren't the bigger issue. The bigger issue was in thinking the old woman had called the police before she'd headed downstairs. Even though local law enforcement weren't exactly overrun with competence, they carried guns.

Still, they'd probably had ten minutes at least before the cops would have shown up. They could have used those ten minutes to search for the map. But instead, they'd both fled the scene like they were being attacked by cougars rather than a bunch of housecats.

He looked up at the third floor again. He'd bet anything that's where the map was. Somewhere in those journals that Sapphire had talked about. He just needed a window of opportunity so that he could get inside the lighthouse and get a peek at those journals. The contractor wasn't going to finish anytime soon, so daytime was out. That was fine by him. It was easier to disappear into the shadows at night.

What he needed was a way to get the girl out of the lighthouse in the middle of the night.

Suddenly, a thought hit him and he smiled.

He knew exactly what he was going to do.

Chapter Six

Zoe was up, showered, pacing her aunt's bedroom, and well into her second pot of coffee before 7:00 a.m. Which was somewhat extraordinary since she hadn't fallen asleep until after three and had done the majority of that sleeping face-planted on the desk in her aunt's bedroom. Not exactly the most comfortable position, and her neck and shoulders were making sure she was aware of it every time she moved. Sometime around five, she'd shuffled over to her aunt's bed and collapsed on top of it, not even bothering with the covers.

She'd been through stacks of journals but so far, there had been no mention of the magic emerald or any other treasure for that matter. Maybe Monte was right and the entire story was hokum. The problem was, how did she get whoever broke into Sapphire's home to believe that as well? Cornelius stood next to the bed and watched as Zoe paused to refill her coffee cup with the last of the second pot she'd brewed.

"You're going to give yourself a heart attack with all that coffee," Cornelius said.

"Right now, this coffee and fear are the only things keeping me awake. I'd prefer it just be the coffee."

Cornelius nodded. "Understandable. Are you worried about speaking to Dane?"

"No. Not at all. I mean, I'm just going to tell the man who I was once involved with that a ghost has verified my intruder theory and that despite the absurdity, they were indeed in search of a magic emerald that likely never existed. What could possibly go wrong with that conversation?"

"You were once involved with Dane?"

Zoe glared at him. "That was your entire take-away from that statement? The whole part where he's going to think I'm nuts because I'm claiming a ghost told me all of that didn't register with you as potentially more important?"

"I suppose so, but there's nothing I can do about that."

Zoe frowned, an idea forming. "Why not? Can't you move something? I mean, even a little flutter of paper would help make my case."

"I'm afraid not. I keep trying, especially when Sapphire bakes, but my hands just pass right through everything I attempt to touch. That's why I don't sit down. I give it a shot every day, but I fall right through chairs."

"You said you sat on the rock at the ocean, and you walk up the stairs in the lighthouse?"

Cornelius shrugged. "I didn't say it makes sense, but that's what I'm working with."

Zoe threw her hands in the air. "You can't touch things, men can't see you, and you can't leave the property. You can't even put on a pair of pants. How the heck are you supposed to help me with anything?"

"I can scare the cats."

"Yeah, because cats never spook."

Cornelius gave her an inquisitive look. "Why would you want me to leave the property?"

"What are you talking about?"

"In your list of my failings, you included the fact that I can't leave the property. What advantage would you have if I could?"

"Easy. If the intruder came back, then you could hop in his truck and go for a ride-along until he took off the mask or went home or both. Then you could identify him."

Cornelius brightened. "Oh, you're right. That would have been very handy."

"Well, we don't have that in our playbook, so we have to stick with what we've got."

"I'm not really sure what that is."

Zoe sighed. "Me either."

The sound of Dane's truck pulling up out front made her stiffen. "He's here."

She put her coffee cup down on the desk and started for the stairs.

"Come with me," she said to Cornelius.

"Why? We've already established there's nothing I can do to help prove my existence."

"I'll think of something," Zoe said, and started down the stairs. She just had to do it in the seconds it took to get to the kitchen.

Dane had unlocked the front door and was walking inside when she stepped into the kitchen. He looked at her in surprise.

"I was afraid I would wake you but I see you're already dressed."

"Sleep and I were not a team last night."

He gave her a sympathetic look. "I didn't figure you would be."

"No worries. Coffee and I are a team this morning and we'll manage to pull it off."

"Maybe after you visit your aunt, you could get some rest. It might be easier during the day...and while I'm here to watch things."

It was something she'd already considered, but Dane's concern made her feel a little warm and fuzzy. It was nice but also uncomfortable.

"Maybe," she said. "Look, there's something I

need to tell you and you have to promise me you won't call me crazy."

He raised his eyebrows. "That is never a good intro for a declaration."

"I know, but it's the one I've got. So?"

He shrugged. "Okay. I won't call you crazy."

Crap. She'd used the wrong terminology and he'd caught it. He would keep his promise not to call her crazy, but he had every right to think it all he wanted.

"There were two men who entered the light-house the night Sapphire fell. They were looking for a map that shows where the emerald is hidden."

His eyes widened. "And you know this how exactly?"

She took a deep breath and began. "This is where the I-promise-I'm-not-crazy part comes in."

She told him about the noise she'd heard the night before and her introduction to Cornelius. Then she went on to relay Cornelius's description of the events the night Sapphire fell. Dane's face remained completely blank, not even so much as a twitch. When she stopped talking and looked at him, he simply stared at her for several uncomfortable seconds.

Finally, he blew out a breath. "I don't even know what to say."

"You promised."

"And I'm trying really hard to keep that promise, but you have got to know how that sounds."

"You've lived in Everlasting your entire life. This whole town is a study in oddities. Are you going to tell me you don't believe any of them?"

Even Zoe had to admit that there were some things in Everlasting she'd never been able to explain with common knowledge. Like Sapphire's affinity with cats.

"Yeah," he said. "There are some strange things that happen here and I don't have a good explanation for all of them, but there's a huge difference between the occasional oddity and claiming a ghost is talking to you."

The anxiety she'd felt ever since she'd awakened shot up several notches, and Zoe struggled to come up with some way to prove to Dane that Cornelius was real. She looked over at Cornelius, who was standing next to the couch, an idea forming.

"Cornelius," she said.

"Wait," Dane interrupted. "You're saying he's standing in this room. Right here? Right now?"

"Yes. He's over by the couch."

Dane squinted at the couch. "Then how come I can't see him?"

"Only women can see him."

"That's kind of sexist, isn't it?"

She threw her hands in the air. "So call your congressman."

She looked back at Cornelius. "Tell me something that you've observed Dane doing when no one else was around to see. Something besides his regular work."

"Like what?" Cornelius asked.

"I don't know what. Something that I wouldn't know or be able to guess."

She glanced over at Dane, who was staring at her with a mixture of concern and disbelief. This whole thing was going about as well as she figured it would.

"Oh," Cornelius said. "He had a roast beef sandwich, sea-salt-and-cracked-pepper potato chips, and grape soda for lunch yesterday. He ate it sitting in the lawn chair out back where he uses his saw during the day."

"Good," Zoe said. "That's good." She repeated what Cornelius said and Dane's eyes widened.

"Okay," he said. "I have no idea how you knew that but I will also say that I eat that same lunch at least three times a week."

"And you think I sought someone out and quizzed them over your lunch habits in order to make you believe I was seeing a ghost?"

He looked uneasy. "No. But Sapphire could have mentioned it."

"I know this might be hard for you to believe, but I don't spend time talking about you when you're not around." She spun around to look at

Cornelius again, then looked back at Dane. "Fine, I have another idea."

She went into the living room and dug a pad of paper and a pen out of an end table, then handed it to Dane. "I want you to go outside and write something on this piece of paper. Anything at all. Cornelius will go with you and read it. Then you'll both come back inside and I'll tell you what it says."

"This is ridiculous," Dane said.

"What can it hurt? At best, you get to prove I'm crazy. I'll even let you say it."

He shook his head. "If it will end this absurd conversation then I'll do it." He headed out the front door and Zoe signaled for Cornelius to follow.

"Close the door," she instructed as Dane walked out, "and make sure the paper is facing the opposite direction of the house. I don't want you coming up with any way that I tricked you."

He shot her one last disbelieving look before pulling the door closed. Cornelius walked right through it and Zoe stood there, fuming and counting the seconds.

About thirty seconds later, Dane walked back inside and stopped a couple of feet in front of her, his arms crossed and a piece of folded paper clutched in his hand.

Zoe looked at Cornelius. "What does the paper say?"

"Aunt Tilly is willy-nilly," Cornelius said. "Is that part of a rhyme? I've never heard it."

Zoe laughed. "It's not a rhyme. It's something Dane used to say about his aunt Tilly when she was stressed."

His eyes widened and she repeated what Cornelius said.

"Do you want to show me the paper?" she asked.

His gaze never left hers as he unfolded the paper and handed it to her. The words she'd just repeated were written on it.

"Now do you believe me?" she asked quietly.

A tiny bit of color had left his face and his mouth hung slightly open. His expression was one of someone who wanted to say something but wasn't quite sure what that something was.

"I, uh…" He walked into the living room and sank onto the couch. Zoe sat next to him, giving him a chance to process the huge curveball he'd just been thrown. She, of all people, knew how it felt.

"I didn't want to believe it either," Zoe said. "I tried to convince myself that I was seeing things, but he was talking, too. Then I pinched myself to make sure I was awake. See, I even have bruises to prove it. Trust me, the absolute last thing in the world I wanted to do was believe that ghosts are real and that one was standing in front of me talking."

Dane ran one hand over his head. "It's incredible and frightening and I don't even know where to begin with my questions, but if I take the existence of the ghost as truth, then my next question is what do you know about him?"

Zoe frowned. "Why does that matter?"

"Because he could be lying about what happened to Sapphire."

"Why in the world would he lie?"

"I don't know, but the reality is we don't know anything about ghosts. But they're not angels, so why would you assume he's perfect? For all you know, this Cornelius could be in cahoots with the guys who broke in here."

Cornelius drew himself up straight and glared at Dane, a completely wasted effort. "I take offense to that. I would never do anything to hurt Sapphire. She's the only friend I have. And on that note, I think I'll take a walk down to the ocean." He looked at Zoe. "Good luck with this narrow-minded cretin."

Zoe winced as Cornelius whirled around and stalked through the wall. "You've hurt his feelings," she said.

Dane's jaw dropped. "I hurt his feelings? Are you listening to yourself?"

"Yes, and although I understand you're being careful, it was still a rude thing to say with him standing right here."

"And how am I supposed to know where he's standing?"

Zoe frowned. "That's a good question. Look, I'll tell you everything I know about Cornelius, but it's going to be what he's told me until I get Sapphire to verify the part of his story that she was involved in."

"Fine. Tell me what you know."

She repeated what she knew about Cornelius to Dane—everything from his murder to the pants situation. He was silent the entire time, and when she was done, he shook his head.

"Never in a million years," he said. "So you believe he's telling the truth?"

"I can't see any reason for him to lie. Think about it. Why would he be in cahoots with a living, breathing thief? What can the living do for a dead person?"

"Assuming he's telling the truth about the people who killed him already being dead and not being able to touch things, then maybe nothing."

"Maybe?"

Dane shrugged. "What if Cornelius thinks the stone can bring him back to life?"

"Now you're being ridiculous."

"It isn't any more far-fetched than anything else, is it? Emerald is the stone of rebirth. Okay, so it doesn't bring him back to life, but what if it can give him power in the afterlife?"

"Like changing clothes, and touching things, and leaving the property?"

Dane nodded. "Why not? Is that any more out there than getting your wish granted for planting a penny in the dirt here? Or any of the other hundred things people in this town believe?"

"When you put it that way…"

Dane leaned close to her and looked directly at her. "Look, I'm not saying this is anything other than what you think. Maybe Cornelius is telling the truth. Maybe he doesn't know anything more about any of this than we do."

"But he might." She sighed. "I'll talk to him. Ask him about the emerald."

"You didn't talk to him about it last night?"

"Not really. I just told him I was reviewing family history and left it at that. Honestly, the whole thing had me kind of creeped out, and I was happy when he left the room."

"Yeah, Jesus, I'm sorry. I hadn't even thought about how you must have felt. Especially being here alone. And I'm sorry I didn't believe you."

"Oh, I wouldn't have believed me either. Not without the dog and pony show. Trust me on that one."

Dane grinned. "What are the odds, right? We might be the only two people in Everlasting who don't buy into the town's claim to fame and here we are, entertaining the thoughts of a ghost."

Zoe closed her eyes and shook her head. "Don't remind me. I'm trying not to think too hard about it because then I'll never dig my way out of that hole. When this is all over, I'll have a nice, long chat with a priest back home and maybe a couple rounds of therapy."

"I was thinking Johnnie Walker Blue Label, but yeah."

"I'm certain I'll never look at a pair of boxer shorts the same way again."

"Me either, and I can't even see him. So what do we do next?"

"The first thing I'm going to do is pick up some breakfast for Sapphire and head to the hospital. And while she eats, I'm going to pick her brain for a list of people she's talked to recently about the emerald and her journals."

He nodded. "Because if someone knew about it before now they would have tried to find the map already."

"Exactly."

Dane checked his watch. "It's only 8:00 a.m. I didn't think visiting hours started until ten."

"They're going to have to get over it. As Sapphire said, one of the things she loves most about me is my ability to ignore stupid rules."

"Do you want me to come with you?"

"No."

He lifted his eyebrows at her quick response.

"I don't want to leave the lighthouse unattended," she explained. "So far, he's only tried to get in at night, but that doesn't mean he wouldn't take a chance during the day if one presented itself."

"That's true," Dane admitted, but she could tell he didn't like it. "Okay. Then I'll keep working. And maybe I'll take a look around a bit in case he's lurking around, waiting on that opportunity you mentioned."

"Be careful with that. Cornelius didn't see any weapons when they were in the lighthouse, but it was dark. It doesn't mean they didn't have any."

"You be careful too," Dane said. "That accident got the original occupant out of the way. The treasure hunters might have expected an empty house at night afterward. But now that you're here and since an accident worked once…"

Zoe nodded and grabbed her purse off the coffee table. She'd worried about someone breaking into the lighthouse again last night, especially after talking to Cornelius, but she hadn't considered that she might be in danger at any opportunity the intruders felt they could seize. Dane's point about getting her out of the way was a good one. She was going to have to be extra careful about where she went and make sure she wasn't being followed. Forcing her econobox rental off the road would be a simple matter for a truck.

The last thing she needed was to end up in a bed in the hospital next to Sapphire.

DANE HAULED a stack of tile out back and set it next to his saw. He glanced around, looking for what, he had no idea, since Cornelius could be standing on his saw table and he wouldn't know it. Which made him sort of queasy. Just the thought that someone, even a dead someone, could be standing around watching him every second was a bit unnerving. Not that he was doing anything that was worthy of gossip, but still. Sometimes a man had to scratch his butt or rearrange things in his jeans. He didn't necessarily want an audience for either.

He grabbed a piece of tile and shook his head, wondering what Zoe was thinking about all of this. She'd discovered him in Sapphire's bedroom last night, which probably meant she was wearing pajamas. At least he hoped she was wearing pajamas. Back when they'd been an item, Zoe had preferred to sleep sans clothes if the weather was warm, and the weather was always warm in California. Hopefully, she'd remembered the brisk October air of Maine when she'd thrown some things in a suitcase and dashed for the plane. Otherwise, Lord only knew what Cornelius had gotten a look at, and

Dane wasn't sure whether to be outraged on Zoe's behalf or disappointed on his own.

He settled on slightly jealous of the ghost and decided he'd leave it at that.

He measured the tile and started to make the cut when he caught something moving in the corner of his eyes off in the woods to his left. He put the tile down and studied the area where he thought he'd seen something, then started walking toward it. About five feet from the tree line, he realized he didn't have anything on him that could serve as a weapon. There was a perfectly good toolbox sitting next to the saw, but he ultimately decided against a retreat and continued into the woods.

He stopped as soon as he set foot in the foliage and listened. Fall winds blew through the trees, loosening dying leaves and sending them fluttering to the ground. He was a good hunter and could easily detect the sound of retreating footsteps, but he didn't hear anything to indicate that someone or something was fleeing the vicinity. It had probably been a bird or maybe a branch falling.

Because he was a good hunter, he was also a skilled tracker, so he walked around the area a bit, looking for signs that something of mass had been in the area. About ten yards away from his original entry point, he found a heel print in a small patch of dirt. The surrounding weeds had been pressed down, indicating that someone had stood there for some time or on more than one occasion. He looked around and started following the signs of passage— a piece of a print here, a broken limb there—until he reached the road. A set of tire tracks marred the otherwise pristine dirt on the shoulder of the road, and he bent down to get a closer look.

Normally, animal tracks were more his speed, but whatever had left this impression was a fairly large tire with a big tread. The kind of tire you'd find on a pickup truck. He took the road back to the lighthouse, not wanting to risk leaving his own prints on the path. Someone had been watching the lighthouse. He was certain. There was no other reason for someone to park in that remote location on the road or walk through the woods to stand in that particular spot unless they wanted to watch the lighthouse without being seen.

Locals and tourists parked on the road on either side of Sapphire's driveway and walked across the lighthouse lawn and down the path to the ocean, sometimes burying a penny on the way or stopping to take photos. But Dane couldn't think of a single good reason for someone to spy on the property. Not a reason that wasn't part of something illegal, anyway.

Despite the fact that he'd changed the locks and installed dead bolts on both doors, he was still worried about Zoe. The windows on the lighthouse were solid, but glass could be cut and a hand inside the opening could easily unlatch one of them. He'd broached the subject of an alarm system with Sapphire but she hadn't seemed interested in discussing it. Granted, until now she hadn't been given a solid reason for it, but Dane thought that given all the strangers who traversed the property every year and the fact that Sapphire wasn't getting any younger, an alarm was a good thing to consider.

Maybe he'd talk to Zoe about it. If he called in a couple of favors he might be able to get equipment within a day. Add another day for installation and Sapphire would probably be secure by the time she got out of the hospital.

In the meantime, he needed to convince Zoe that she needed added protection. He knew there was no way she'd leave the lighthouse for a hotel, but maybe he could convince her to let him stay there with her. He'd give it a shot, anyway.

If she said no, then he'd think of something else.

Like maybe sleeping in his truck on her front lawn.

Chapter Seven

Zoe marched into the hospital with purpose. She'd been told once that as long as you looked like you knew what you were doing and didn't make eye contact, most people wouldn't question you. But instead of Dour Debbie at the front desk, the smiling Mary Jo greeted her.

"Good morning," the nurse said. "You're out early."

"I know it's not visiting hours yet, but I need to sneak Sapphire some edible food and get some information from her about the lighthouse. It's important."

Mary Jo waved her hand in dismissal. "Ms. Sapphire's been up for hours already. I don't care if you go back there. And I completely understand the food thing." She looked behind her to make sure no other employees were around, then leaned forward and lowered her voice. "I've been known to bring my favorite patients cinnamon rolls. Ms. Sapphire might have already had one."

Zoe smiled. She really liked Mary Jo.

"Don't tell me they have you working a double?" Zoe said.

"Sort of. The nurse who works the day shift is ill so they asked me to cover part of her shift since last night I wasn't on rotation. Then I get to go home and get some sleep before I cover my own shift tonight."

"Ugh. That's brutal."

"It's all right. I like the overtime. It keeps me in bath salts and massages."

"At least you've got priorities. How's Sapphire doing?"

"Fantastic," Mary Jo said. "I came in today thinking I'd find her improved but she's really exceeded expectation. When you consider her age, she's really a wonder. If I were just looking at charts, I'd guess her to be a good twenty years younger than she is."

"She's definitely tapped into the fountain of youth."

Mary Jo nodded. "I'm sure you talked to Dr. Prescott yesterday about her test results, but I couldn't believe how much the swelling had gone down. There's hardly any left."

"Really? I talked to the doctor after he got the

results and he said there was improvement but he didn't seem as happy about it as you are."

Mary Jo rolled her eyes. "Don't tell anyone I said it, but it's the lawyers. They've got doctors afraid to commit to anything positive. Heck, Sapphire could be doing Olympic-level gymnastics down the hallways and they'd still hedge on their opinion."

"State of the world, I suppose. The news station I work for got sued because the weather prediction was for sunshine. At the last minute, and based on that prediction, a bride moved her wedding outside and it poured."

"Good Lord Almighty. What will people think of next?"

Given that Zoe was currently dealing with a ghostly roommate and a set of intruders who believed a magic emerald was hidden somewhere on her aunt's property, she wasn't about to answer that question. Mary Jo would call for a straitjacket.

"I'm sure they'll think of something worse," Zoe said. "It was nice talking to you, and thanks again for letting me break the rules. And for looking out for Sapphire."

"Of course."

Zoe headed to Sapphire's room, already bracing for the situation she knew was coming. She was thrilled to hear Mary Jo's report of Sapphire's condition but also knew that if her aunt felt that good, she'd be itching to get back home. Zoe wanted her aunt back in her own home as much as Sapphire did, but with everything going on, she couldn't help but think Sapphire might be safer staying where she was.

When she walked into the room, she came to an abrupt halt and stared. Sapphire was standing on her hospital bed, eyes closed, bent over at the waist with her hands on the bed, forming a perfect triangle. If the entire situation hadn't sent anxiety coursing through her, Zoe would have taken a second or two to be impressed.

"What in the world are you doing?" Zoe rushed over to the bed, ready to catch her aunt if she lost her balance and fell to the side. She just hoped it was the side of the bed she was on.

Sapphire let out a deep breath, sank onto her knees, then opened her eyes and smiled at Zoe. "I was doing downward dog. I've been harping on you for years to take up yoga. You see what kind of shape I'm in. I'm going to live to be a hundred."

"I'm sure that's true, but can you try not to give me a heart attack while doing it?"

In one fluid move, Sapphire pulled her legs out from under her body and grabbed the remote to lift the upper body portion of the bed. Okay. Maybe when Zoe got back to LA she'd sign up for a class. It shouldn't be hard to find one. Basically, all she had to do was throw a rock and she'd hit a building with a yoga studio.

"How are things at the lighthouse?" Sapphire asked. "How are the cats?"

"The kitchen is coming along and I checked out the rest of the remodeling last night. The master suite is to die for. If I could have food delivery up to the third floor, I'm not sure I'd ever leave."

Sapphire beamed. "It is beautiful, isn't it? The view was always incredible, of course, looking out over the ocean, but now the inside matches the outside."

"Yes, and when I went up there last night after my shower, I met Cornelius."

"So you *can* see him! I knew you'd be able to."

Zoe frowned. "He said women could see him. Last time I checked, I had all the right plumbing."

"Some women can see him, but not all. And if he doesn't want you to see him, you won't. That silly Polly Crawford has a crush on him and is always dressing up when she makes an excuse to drop by, so he refuses to let her see him."

"Really? That's interesting. Not the part about Polly—that's just sad—but the other part. That some people can't see him. I wonder why?"

"Most of the local women who've been to the lighthouse since he showed up can see him just fine, but the tourists walk right by him. I think there's something about being from Everlasting that makes it possible. Something inherited."

Zoe hesitated. "Magic?"

"Maybe. What's wrong with a little magic?"

"If it produces talkative, half-dressed ghosts, then maybe a lot."

Sapphire smiled. "There is that."

"Cornelius told me his story, about his cousin and his wife. He said you checked on them for him."

"It's the first thing I did after he told me the story. It took a bit to run them down. The older records aren't online and since they'd left the area, I didn't know where to start looking. A nice girl at the library who's into genealogy helped me, and I found their deaths recorded in a church Bible that contained a family tree for all the founding members."

"The branch Cornelius and his cousin were on must have looked a bit odd, sharing a wife and all."

Sapphire frowned. "There was no mention of that in the book. It was a Bible, after all."

"And it might have gone up in flames if the truth was recorded?"

"My guess is the entry was left sterile in order to protect the dignity of Cornelius."

"Oh. I can see that. So his story is true?"

"Why wouldn't it be?"

"I don't know. I guess I just wanted to be certain that I can trust what he says. I mean, if we're going to go ahead and admit that ghosts exist, why do we have to assume that they leave all worldly emotions behind? I figure Cornelius can be mad or sad or happy or bored and if all that's true, then he's as capable as the living of lying or manipulating to get his way."

Sapphire stared at her for several seconds, then blinked. "That's absolutely fascinating, and I'd never really considered it. You're right, of course. Or at least, I think you are because it makes sense. But to address your original concern, I've never had any reason to believe Cornelius has lied to me and in all the time he's been with me, he's never given me any reason to suspect him of nefarious intent."

It was as good a guarantee as Zoe was going to get, so she'd have to take it. So would Dane, for that matter, because the ghost wasn't going anywhere. Zoe took in a breath, trying to figure out how to broach the next subject with her aunt. She had narrowed it down to two different approaches when Sapphire squeezed her arm.

"Just say it," Sapphire said. "I'm a tough old broad. I don't need protecting and I want to know what's going on."

"Okay." Zoe told Sapphire everything Cornelius had told her about the intruders. "I think the sleeping pill is probably affecting your memory as well as the fall. Those things are pretty potent."

"You're probably right. I didn't want to take

them, but I was having so much trouble sleeping. And Dr. Prescott kept insisting that I had to do something, so I finally agreed to try them out. I'd only been taking them a couple nights. I will admit, I slept without stirring even a bit, but I don't think I'll be taking more of them."

"I think that's probably a good idea, especially now." Zoe then went on to describe Dane's conversation with Sam and Monte. "Do you know the story about the magic emerald?"

"Of course. And I've told it to you before." Sapphire frowned. "If you didn't automatically dismiss everything you can't prove, you might have paid more attention."

"I'm a scientist," Zoe said, the same tired argument popping out before she could stop it.

"And yet the weather does unexpected things all the time, like that downpour that you got caught in yesterday."

"That's because we still don't know enough to predict everything, but that doesn't mean when the unexpected happens it's without explanation."

"There's an explanation for magic as well. It's just not part of traditional belief systems. Neither are ghosts, but you sat right here relaying a conversation to me that you had with one. How does that compute with your narrow worldview?"

"I don't know and I don't want to think about it right now. I need for you to be safe. That's all I care about. I can have a nervous breakdown afterward."

Sapphire gave her a sympathetic look. "I'm sorry. I know this must all be difficult for you, and I'm not making it any better by trying to push you harder toward the way I see things. You've made my safety your priority, and that should be enough for me to shut my mouth unless it's saying 'thank you.'"

"You don't have to thank me. You're my family. I'd do anything to protect you."

"You're a good girl, Zoe. You always were. A bit challenging to someone who thinks the way I do, but you never let our differences of opinion cloud your love for me. A lot of people would have."

"A lot of people are fools."

"Yes. Well, that's another discussion for another day. A day that includes lots of wine."

"It might have to happen sooner than you expect, because although you might not think it's foolish to believe in a magic emerald, it *is* beyond foolish to break into the lighthouse to steal from you."

"Foolish, desperate...sometimes they promote the same action."

"Have you told the story to anyone recently? Someone who might not have heard it before?"

Sapphire's brow wrinkled in thought and finally her eyes widened. "Yes. I told the story at a charity dinner for the hospital about a week ago. They're trying to build a cancer ward for children. Such a good cause."

"And that dinner is the only time you can remember telling the story, say, in the last two weeks?"

Sapphire nodded. "You know how it is around here—the old-timers either don't want to hear that sort of thing or they've already heard it and don't want to hear it again. And young people always have something to do when they see one of us oldies approaching. They don't want to get caught in the midst of one of our reminiscing bouts. Some people think it's rude, but I don't blame them. They're young and have jobs and kids and houses to tend to. What little free time they have, they don't want to spend it listening to a bunch of old people with long winded tales."

Because Zoe had been known to cross the street just to avoid some of the worst of the Everlasting gasbags, she remained wisely quiet on the subject.

"Can you remember who was at the dinner?" Zoe asked, steering the conversation back to the topic at hand.

"Not all of them, I'm afraid. There were a hundred tickets sold. It was a barbecue, so easy to feed a large crowd."

Zoe's optimism took a big hit. If her aunt had flitted around the event telling the story, that still left her with ninety-nine direct suspects plus anyone they might have relayed the story to.

"But you don't need to know them all," Sapphire continued. "I told the story while we were eating. There were only twelve people per table and one seat was empty.

"Do you remember who the others were?"

"Of course. I'm not so ancient my mind can't hold on to the names of ten people I just shared a meal with. Let's see...Father Malcolm, Ralph and Rhonda Simmons, Trevor and Martha Piedmont, Sheriff Bull and one of those silly boy toys she's hired, the Belmont brothers, and Mary Jo."

Zoe mulled over the list. Six men. Cornelius had been certain the voices and the bodies did not belong to women, so that left out Rhonda, Martha, Sheriff Bull, and Mary Jo as potential suspects. At least, they weren't one of the people who broke into the lighthouse. They could have repeated the story elsewhere, but Zoe could only manage so much at once. She'd start with these six men and see what she could find. If that turned up nothing, then she'd branch out.

"Do you know which one of Sheriff Bull's boy toys was with her?"

Sapphire shook her head. "But if you bring in the calendar, I could probably point him out."

"I don't suppose you have one of those calendars."

"Lord no! But you can buy a copy down at the sheriff's department."

"Lovely." She could hardly wait to run that errand.

"You can't think…" Sapphire said. "I mean, none of those people would break into my home. They all live here—some of their families have been here for several generations."

Zoe hadn't held out much hope that her aunt would be good at pointing out the bad guy. Sapphire never wanted to believe the worst of people, especially people from Everlasting.

"I know you don't want to believe that," Zoe said, "but someone did break into your house, and thanks to Cornelius, we know it was about the emerald."

"But that story has been around for years. And it's not one of the popular ones, so why break in now?"

"Because whoever broke in just heard it."

"Oh. That's why you asked me who I'd told the story to recently." Sapphire gave her an appreciative look. "You're a smart girl, with so much ability. More ability than you even know. One day…"

Before her aunt could launch off into the many blessings Zoe might have inherited from her supposedly gifted ancestors, she rose from the chair and gave her aunt a kiss.

"You leaving already?" Sapphire asked.

"I have some alibis to check and I need to pick up your lunch and dinner and apparently, a calendar. Is there anything in particular that you want to eat?"

"You did a great job yesterday. I'm fine with you picking again."

"Okay. Then I'll be back around noon."

Zoe headed out of the hospital, giving Mary Jo a wave on her way out.

She recognized a few of the people that Sapphire had named, but six years allowed for a lot of changes. She needed to get back to the lighthouse and go over the names with Dane. He'd know which ones to start with. Then once they had an order to investigate them in, she'd figure out how to do that.

She had a thirty-minute drive to come up with something.

DESPITE HIS STROLL in the woods and the constant mental distraction of looking for a ghost he couldn't see, Dane managed to finish tiling the kitchen floor. He was sitting in a lawn chair out back when Zoe stepped around the side of the lighthouse.

"The floor looks great," she said. "I didn't walk on it."

Figuring she must have seen the slight look of

panic when she'd mentioned the floor, he nodded. "Thanks."

She glanced around, then looked back at him. "Can we go inside and talk? I don't really want to discuss things out here."

"Sure." He rose from the chair and followed her around the lighthouse and inside, then plopped down on the couch. "How is Sapphire?"

"She's good. Really good."

"Even after you told her what Cornelius said."

"Yeah. I mean, she's concerned but I think she always knew there was someone in the lighthouse, even though she couldn't remember it."

"Probably. It's still embedded in her mind somewhere. Did you ask her about the emerald?"

"Yes, and also about Cornelius." She repeated what Sapphire had said about the ghost. "I know it still doesn't prove that Cornelius is being truthful, but she believes he is and well, so do I. But I can't give you a good reason why and I definitely can't offer you proof."

He nodded. "If you and Sapphire both think he's being honest then I'll go with your instincts. You can see and hear him, which allows you to study body language and inflection. I don't have that perspective."

Zoe blinked and he could tell she was surprised that he acquiesced so easily, but he'd already mulled the entire thing over while finishing the floor. The reality was even if the ghost was lying, it didn't really change anything. He was certain someone had been in the lighthouse because he knew someone had been watching it. What other reason could someone have for standing in that spot in the woods other than assessing what his opportunities for entry were?

"Awesome," Zoe finally said. "So the emerald… Sapphire told the story at some benefit dinner for the hospital."

"I remember that. I sent a donation but didn't go. I was finishing up the master bathroom and didn't want to take the time. I heard the dinner sold out, though. If Sapphire told the story there, then there's no telling how many people are walking around with that information."

"Well, I've got it narrowed down to six to start, because Sapphire said she told it at the table while they were eating. Eleven people at her table, so ten people other than her, and four were women. I know someone at the table could have told someone else and so forth, but we have to start somewhere, and six is manageable."

"Makes sense. Give me the names."

Zoe repeated the names and Dane considered each one as she spoke. When she was done, he nodded.

"Okay. The good news is, I can eliminate two right off the bat. Trevor Piedmont is in a wheelchair as a result of a car accident a couple years ago. And Father Malcolm was at a convention in Florida. He came back yesterday with a tan to prove it."

"A tan in October. That's solid evidence that he wasn't in Maine. Great, so that leaves Ralph Simmons, one of the calendar boys, and the Belmont brothers. I vaguely remember the Simmonses—older couple. He was always yelling at people to get away from his roses."

Dane nodded. "Simmons is very serious about his roses and little else. He's a retired horticulturist. Mixes his own soil. Makes his own fertilizer."

"Has anyone had problems with him?"

"He was arrested for assault this past summer. A tourist broke a rose off one of his bushes and proposed to his girlfriend right there on the sidewalk. Simmons stormed out of his house, slapped the guy right across the face, and took the rose from the girl."

"What did she say?"

"Huh?"

"The girl. Did she say yes to marrying the rose thief?"

He frowned. "I have no idea. Does that matter?"

"Probably only to girls. Okay, so Simmons has a mean streak if he wants to."

"Yeah, but my money is on the Belmont brothers."

"Why is that? I don't recognize the name."

"Patrick and Frank Belmont are the grandsons of Patricia Moore."

Zoe perked up. "I know that name. My mom went to school with her daughter Amber."

"Yes, well, Amber didn't turn out as productive as your mother. She ran off with a truck driver and had the two boys. My understanding is the trucker slapped her around some until finally dumping her for a newer model. She had developed a drug habit to deal with the beatings, so she sent the boys to live with their grandmother."

"Then they must be about our age, right?"

"A few years younger. They didn't show up in Everlasting until you were in college, which is probably why you didn't run across them. They fit the description—both fairly tall and one thinner while the other has a bit more mass."

"And I'm guessing they're trouble."

"Nothing but. They still live with their grandmother because they couldn't hold a job for more than a couple weeks. Everyone who hired them got burned. They didn't show up for work and when they did, the work was sloppy. They stole from several employers."

"Why aren't they in jail?"

"Small town. No one wants to press charges because they feel sorry for Patricia, but everyone wishes they'd take a hike out of here. I don't see it happening, though. Not as long as they have free room and board."

"I don't recall Patricia being overly flush with money. It can't be much of a life if three people are living off what she has. For that matter, why would they be at a charity dinner? Doesn't sound like the sort of thing they'd go in for, especially when you pay far more for the food than it's worth."

"My guess is Patricia was given a couple free tickets. She's a cancer survivor and does volunteer work with children at the hospital. She probably passed them along to the brothers, who figured a free meal was a free meal."

"That's one meal, but what about all the rest? They can't just sit on a couch all day eating ramen noodles."

"They do odd jobs when people will hire them. Day labor for lawn work, moving furniture. Willie tried using them a couple times before he hired me, but they stole his tools and the work they did was so shoddy, it all had to be redone."

He frowned. "It's interesting what you say about money, though, because every time I'm in the Magic Eight Ball, they are too."

"Then they must have a source of cash."

"A buddy of mine lives a couple towns over. He said they've had a rash of break-ins lately. The thieves took things easy to pawn—televisions, computers, jewelry—and of course, cash. The description of the thieves fits the men who broke into the lighthouse, down to the dark-colored pickup truck."

"Maybe the brothers are smart enough to do their illegal activities outside of Everlasting. With Sheriff Bull's band of boy toys in charge of law enforcement in the area, I can't imagine a lot of crime is getting solved."

"Probably not. I'm starting to hear rumbling about the next election, especially from men. Sheriff Bull and her boys might be looking for another modeling gig."

"That might be a good thing if February is the smartest of the lot."

"Sorry about that. I guess I gave him more credit than he was due."

"Not your fault. Okay, so let's assume the Belmont brothers are our best bet. They might be doing some thieving already in other towns, but they heard about the emerald and thought they'd risk the local action for the potentially big score."

"If that emerald is the size people say it is, it would set someone up for life. Maybe not them, in particular, as they'd probably manage to blow through any amount of money quickly, but for most people, it would be a very nice retirement plan."

"So how do we figure out if it was them? I mean, we can't exactly knock on Patricia's door and ask if they were in bed the night Sapphire fell."

"She probably wouldn't know anyway. My guess is she's already figured out the less she knows about where they are and what they're doing, the better off she is."

"Probably. So any other ideas?"

"Maybe. I'll stop by the Magic Eight Ball tonight and put some feelers out. No one likes the brothers much, so if anyone has even an inkling that they had something to do with Sapphire's fall, they'll tell me."

"If someone knew, wouldn't they report it to the police?"

"Not if they hadn't made the connection. The brothers aren't foolish enough to talk straight out about breaking into a house, but they might be running their mouth about coming into money or leaving town."

Zoe nodded. "That makes sense. Then the only one left on the list to identify is which deputy was at the table."

"How do you plan on doing that?"

"As much as it pains me, when I go downtown to pick up Sapphire's meals, I will purchase a calendar, then she can pick him out."

Dane smiled. "You're going to buy a calendar?"

"Do you have a better suggestion? That's the most efficient way to get a picture of all of them in front of Sapphire. Unless you want to buy the calendar, I can't think of a better option."

He put his hands up in the air, slightly horror-struck at the suggestion. "Your plan works."

"I thought so." She grabbed her purse and keys. "Then I'm going to get to it."

"Wait! Before you go, there's something else."

Zoe instantly stiffened. "What is it?"

"I did a perimeter search earlier," he said, and went on to explain what he'd found and what he thought it implied.

"We figured they might be watching," she said.

"Yea, but thinking something might be happening is different from knowing it is."

"Boy, isn't that the truth. If they've been watching, they might know I called the sheriff's department. They could have seen me talking to February. Do you think they'd risk breaking in again?"

"I just don't know. Maybe they'll wait until you leave and Sapphire's back in place. You're an unknown, and Sapphire would be easier to constrain if it went that far. Or if they're really patient, maybe they'll wait for me to finish my work and break in one day when Sapphire leaves to run errands. That would be the smart thing to do."

"But your description didn't make them sound overly smart."

"Smart and patient are two different things. They'd need to be both to wait it out."

"I don't like this. We have to figure out what's

going on or Sapphire won't be safe in her own home, and I can't live with that."

"Neither can I." He put his hand on her arm and gave it a light squeeze. "We're going to fix this."

Just that tiny bit of contact sent a rush of memories flooding through him, and he removed his hand before he did something they'd both regret.

"Thank you for your help," she said. "I couldn't do this without you."

"You can do most anything by yourself. You've proven that."

"Not this. I need your help to make Sapphire safe, and you know it's not easy for me to admit that sort of thing. So please, take the compliment and let me leave before I embarrass myself further."

"Some things never change."

She nodded and headed out the door.

He sighed.

No. Some things definitely never did.

Chapter Eight

Zoe arrived back at the hospital to raised voices and a very angry aunt. Sapphire sat upright in her bed, her face flushed and pointing her finger at Dr. Prescott.

"That's crap, and you know it," Sapphire said. "I'm perfectly fine. Hell, most fifty-year-olds would kill to be in the shape I'm in."

"I'm sure that's true," Dr. Prescott said, "but the fact is, you're not fifty and that means we have to take less risk with your recovery, not more."

"You said the swelling was gone," Sapphire argued.

"That doesn't mean the injury is healed," Dr. Prescott said. "Can you remember what happened that night?"

Sapphire crossed her arms across her chest.

"No. But what does that matter? I took one of those sleeping pills. I might never remember."

"It's just one more day," Dr. Prescott said. "If everything is the same or better tomorrow, then I'll discharge you tomorrow afternoon." He glanced over at Zoe with a slightly pleading look.

Zoe walked up to the side of the bed and looked at her aunt. "One more day won't kill you," she said. "And it will give me and Dr. Prescott peace of mind."

"I know my own body better than either of you," Sapphire said, but Zoe could tell she was close to giving up the argument.

"Of course you do," Zoe said. "Which is why I said you staying another day was for my benefit and for Dr. Prescott's. Plus, that would give Dane one more day of work before you get home. I think he said the appliances arrive tomorrow. You might come home to a usable kitchen. Wouldn't that be a treat?"

"I *am* looking forward to seeing the finished product," Sapphire said, somewhat mollified. Finally, she sighed. "Fine. If it makes all of you feel better, then I'll give it one more day, but unless I have a major medical crisis between now and tomorrow, I expect to be sleeping in my own bed tomorrow night."

"I don't see any reason why you won't be," Dr. Prescott said. He gave Zoe a nod and left the room.

Sapphire watched him go and shook her head. "He's overprotective."

"He's a doctor. Isn't he supposed to be overprotective?"

"He didn't used to be. I mean, he's always gotten onto me about the things I do. Like washing the windows on the lighthouse. He said I should hire someone to do it for me. That I have no business hauling a bucket of water up and down an extension ladder."

Zoe totally agreed with the doctor on that one but wasn't about to argue with her aunt. Mainly because there was no future in it, and because agreeing with Dr. Prescott might make Sapphire less amenable to catering to Zoe's own overprotectiveness.

"Well, this time you ended up in the hospital," Zoe said. "He's naturally worried. And head injuries aren't exactly a scrape or bruise. You never know what can happen."

"Maybe. But I'd bet my last dollar that if this had happened a year ago, he would have sent me home sooner."

"What happened to change things a year ago?" Zoe asked.

"He was diagnosed with cancer. He doesn't ever talk about it, but I know he's the big push behind the new cancer ward for kids."

"Really? He looks in good shape to have cancer."

Sapphire nodded. "I assume his treatments are going well. He hasn't even lost his hair...I mean what he had left of it. It's been thinning ever since I met him. Anyway, ever since his diagnosis, he's been more cautious."

"I guess that makes sense, facing his own mortality and all. Maybe you should give him a break then."

"I *am* giving him a break. If I'd been my usual self, this argument would have happened yesterday."

Zoe grinned. "Fair enough. Well, if you're ready to get off your high horse, I have vegetable soup and blueberry scones."

Sapphire clapped her hands. "I'm so glad I let you pick."

Zoe pulled the food out of a paper bag and sat it on the tray in front of her aunt. Then she reached back inside the bag and pulled out the calendar.

"And I have this," she said. "You have no idea how embarrassing this was to purchase."

Sapphire glanced at the calendar and grimaced. "The whole thing is an embarrassment to the county, law enforcement everywhere, and the taxpaying citizens who have to suffer this mess."

"I got catcalls," Zoe said.

"Catcalls?"

"I made the mistake of stopping to pick up the

calendar first. They didn't have a bag to put it in, so I got to walk all the way to the deli holding this thing. Every male on the sidewalk tried to explain why he was a better pick or how if I was desperate, I could take it down a notch and roll with him. I practically ran the entire length of downtown."

Sapphire laughed. "The festival people must be in good spirits. Okay, show me that nonsense and let's get this over with. I need to eat, and dwelling on it for any longer than necessary could ruin my appetite."

Zoe flipped open the calendar to January and started the show of shame. Unfortunately, it wasn't until September that her aunt stopped her.

"Wait," Sapphire said. "I think that's him."

"Are you sure?"

"Not completely sure. I mean, he looks different with clothes on, but I know he had dark hair and blue eyes, and the face is the only one that's seemed more familiar to me."

"Dane said September was Sheriff Bull's favorite, so you're probably right."

"She has a favorite?" Sapphire asked, clearly dismayed. "And people know about it?"

"I'm afraid so."

Sapphire shook her head. "So does that mean you still think it was one of the people at the table?"

"That's the theory we're running with. Dane's betting on the Belmont brothers."

"Given their dubious life choices, they are probably the most likely, which is unfortunate since their grandmother is such a nice woman. I guess I never saw them as having that much initiative, but I've been wrong about people before."

Zoe tried not to make a face. That was the understatement of the century. Sapphire was Miss Congeniality. For someone who had introverted tendencies, she rarely met a person she didn't like, and they had to go above and beyond in the opposite direction before she changed her mind. She gave the expression "giving people the benefit of the doubt" whole new meaning.

"Dane's going to the Magic Eight Ball tonight to try to run down some gossip on them," Zoe said.

"I wish I weren't tied to this bed," Sapphire said. "I could be out helping you two."

"What I need your help with is the emerald. Are you sure there's nothing in the journals that references the stone or where it was hidden?"

"If I'd found anything of the sort, don't you think I would have looked for the stone myself? If someone else finds it, it would be a huge loss to Everlasting. All the magic in the town links back to that stone. If it's removed, everything could change."

"You really believe the magic could disappear?"

Sapphire nodded.

Zoe held in a sigh. "And there's nowhere else

you can think of that a map or references to the stone might exist?"

"Not in anything I own. Those journals are the only old documents I have. None of my furniture dates back that far, so no hidden compartments with treasure maps are likely."

"What about Wilber? Do you think he might have something at his shop?"

Wilber Messing was a retired paranormal researcher and owned the Hunted Treasures Antiques & Artifacts Shop. Now he sold antiques and artifacts but kept the ones he thought had the ability to harm people locked away and under close watch.

Sapphire shook her head. "If Wilber had anything of the sort, he would have discussed it with me a long time ago. The founders' ancestors stick together on that sort of thing."

"So the Fraternal Order of Light probably wouldn't know anything either." Zoe remembered hearing about the international artifact hunters before but wasn't sure what their knowledge and access consisted of.

"With no ancestors in their group, I can't imagine they would."

"Could anyone else have journals? Some other descendant of the original inhabitants? A distant cousin, maybe?"

Sapphire thought for a minute. "Harriet Wilson might have something."

Zoe blinked. "Harriet Wilson? She's still alive?"

Sapphire waved a hand in dismissal. "She cruised right past ninety and kept going. The old bat is probably going to live to be a thousand and keeps getting less pleasant every year."

Zoe knew Harriet Wilson well. Every kid who had ever made the mistake of walking across her lawn knew who she was, because she took that opportunity to turn her water hose on them, regardless of how cold it was. In later years, she upgraded to a huge water pistol for portability and accuracy—at least that's what she told law enforcement when complaints were made. If Harriet was even less pleasant now than she was back then, she might have sprouted horns and a tail.

"Well, it's not likely that she would help me," Zoe said.

Sapphire frowned for a minute, then brightened. "She might, but you have to pitch it the right way. Tell her that you're here visiting me and I'm claiming that my family is responsible for bringing magic to Everlasting and that when I die it will all disappear. Tell her I said she had documents to prove it."

"And what exactly will that accomplish?"

"Oh, it will piss her off. Harriet is certain her family is responsible for the magic in Everlasting and if she has something that might prove otherwise, she won't be able to resist shoving it in your face."

"Great."

She'd already planned on paying Ralph Simmons a visit. Now she could add Harriet Wilson to the list. The thought of the blissful nap she'd planned disappeared and was replaced with what was certain to be a long afternoon of people yelling at her.

Another glorious day in Everlasting.

ON THE DRIVE back to downtown, Zoe worked on the speech that she planned to use on Ralph Simmons. It was all a bunch of elaborate hooey about how depressed Sapphire was and how Zoe knew he had the best roses in the state and if he could just sell her a couple for a nice bud vase then she knew it would make Sapphire's day.

The conversation, of course, was meaningless, but she needed something to get her foot in the door, so to speak. If she could get Simmons talking, then she might be able to assess his level of crazy and determine if it extended beyond his front lawn.

The Simmons house was two blocks off Main Street, but despite that distance, the street already contained a fair number of cars that Zoe guessed did not belong to residents. She squeezed her rental into a space two doors down from Simmons and started up the sidewalk to his house. When she was about ten yards away, he came around the side of the house, carrying a bucket and a pair of pruning shears.

Score one for efficiency. He was already outside and about to work on the roses.

"Hi, Mr. Simmons," she said as she approached the white picket fence. She'd used her perkiest voice and plastered on a big smile.

Simmons glanced up at her without comment and then turned his attention back to the rosebush in front of him. His eyes were watery and his nose was slightly red, as if he'd been blowing it often.

"Mr. Simmons," she said again as she stepped up right on the other side of the fence from him. "It's Zoe Parker—Sapphire Parker's niece."

He kept cutting, not even sparing a glance at her. "I know who you are. That scoundrel you used to date stole a rose from my bushes on prom night to take to you."

"Oh wow. I'm sorry. I didn't know."

"You do now."

Zoe blinked, no idea where to go with this conversation now. Clearly, any talk of asking for roses was out of the question, and what was Dane thinking, not giving her fair warning that he'd stolen from Simmons before?

"Well, that was a long time ago, and I'm sure he's sorry," she said. "Anyway, I don't know if you heard but Sapphire fell and is in the hospital."

"I heard. The old fool needs to sell that place and get a one-story."

"Yes, well, she's been doing some remodeling at the lighthouse and I thought it would be nice to get her a rosebush for her sitting garden. I've never seen roses as beautiful as yours, so I thought I'd ask your advice on what to get."

The clipping finally stopped and he stared intently at her, as if trying to determine if she was serious or if her words were all part of some nefarious plot to steal one of his roses and run for the hills. She tried to look as pleasant, earnest, and honest as she was capable of and after several uncomfortable seconds, he finally sniffed and nodded.

"A bush is always a better gift than a vase of flowers," he said. "If properly cared for it can produce beautiful blooms long beyond the life of its owner. I don't know Sapphire's skill level, so I would suggest starting with a simpler variety to care for and one that will thrive in sandy soil, perhaps *Rosa rugosa*, commonly referred to as the beach rose. If she wants to invest more time in her landscaping and less in those godforsaken animals she's filled her house up with, then she can add something more challenging."

"I take it you're not a fan of cats?"

"Of course not! I'm allergic and they can tear up a flower bed in a matter of minutes with their quarreling. A darn nuisance if you ask me."

"They can be a handful. Hey, do you still have that old black Cadillac? That car was in perfect condition."

"Unfortunately, no. Some drunken hooligans ran into it when I was parked at the post office. Insurance said it wasn't worth fixing. I argued, of course, but couldn't change their mind. I have a pickup truck now. It's not as comfortable, but it's better for hauling plants."

"I'm sorry to hear that. It was a really nice car. Well, thank you for your time and your advice, Mr. Simmons. I'll let you get back to your roses."

He had already returned to his work before the first two words left her mouth and didn't so much as glance up as she began to walk away. As soon as her back was turned, she blew out a breath. Holy crap! Disgruntled old Simmons might be one of the thieves. The watery eyes and runny nose could be from coming in contact with Sapphire's cats, and he drove a pickup truck. She just needed to verify the color, but for the moment, Simmons was at the top of the list.

As she walked down the sidewalk, her cell phone rang. The number in the display had her back and neck tightening. She stopped walking and took the call from her boss, praying he wasn't about to tell her things she didn't want to hear.

"Parker," he said. "When will you be back?"

She knew there was no point, but she still bristled. "My aunt is doing well, thank you for asking."

"Uh, that's nice. So you'll be on the next plane to LA then."

"I'm afraid not. She's still in the hospital and I can't leave until she's released and I'm certain she's okay being alone."

There was silence on the other end for a bit and she steeled herself for what she was certain was coming.

"The position opened up. Pamela's already interviewed and you know what that means. My bosses want to close a deal as quickly as possible and they won't even consider you without talking to you."

Zoe struggled to fight back the tears that were forming. "They won't consider me anyway unless I'm offering up the same skill set as Pamela."

The office rumor was that Pamela had made the rounds in the executive lounge a time or two. She was blonde and plastic with fake boobs and a fake smile. She didn't have half the knowledge Zoe had and didn't seem to care about it, but then apparently, she didn't have to.

"Isn't there something you can do?" Zoe asked.

"You know how long I've been waiting for this opportunity and how hard I've been working."

He sighed. "If I had my way, we'd have fired that idiot brother-in-law of the CEO and you'd have been on the air years ago. But you know how it is."

The resignation in his voice had her tears to the point of bursting loose. Her boss was so abrupt people often took him as rude, but he knew talent. And before the station had been bought out by a big conglomerate, he'd had an excellent staff with great credentials, but those days were long gone. Somewhere deep down, Zoe had always known it would come to this. That she was grasping for something that no longer existed. That politics and who you knew, biblically and otherwise, were what got you ahead…not actual talent.

But it still sucked to hear it.

"Zoe?" he asked. "You still there?"

"I'm sorry," she said. "I can't leave."

"I would have been surprised to hear you say anything else. I'm really sorry, Zoe."

"So am I," she said.

As soon as she disconnected, the dam burst.

Chapter Nine

Zoe had a good cry in her rental car and got a few concerned stares from festivalgoers, but fortunately, no one had felt the need to knock on the window and ask her what was wrong. She wiped her nose with a napkin from the coffee shop and checked her face in the rearview mirror. Her eyes and nose looked as bad as Mr. Simmons's had. She pulled a tube of tinted moisturizer out of her purse and rubbed it on, then reassessed. The blotchy red spots still showed through the light cream but it was a little better. At least some of the redness in her eyes was starting to fade away.

Maybe by the time she got to Harriet Wilson's house, she'd look semi-normal.

She started the car and drove a couple blocks away from downtown to the house where Harriet's family had lived for three generations. It was an old

Victorian and had been painted an old and unattractive shade of yellow when Zoe lived in Everlasting, and as she pulled up to the curb, she saw that hadn't changed. In fact, Harriet had doubled down on the ugly yellow because two men were outside painting.

Zoe got out of the car and headed up the walkway to the house. The two men painting both stopped working to give her an up-and-down. She gave them a quick nod and picked up her pace. She was no stranger to being stared at and had even had her share of catcalls, but something about those looking her over created the strong sense of needing to shower. She stepped onto the porch and rang the doorbell. There were footsteps inside and the door flew open, and Harriet Wilson glared at her.

"You're interrupting my game shows," Harriet said. "What do you want?"

"Mrs. Wilson, I'm Zoe Parker. I don't know if you remember me."

Harriet narrowed her eyes. "Sapphire Parker's niece. I can't imagine what you're doing on my doorstep because if it has anything to do with Sapphire, it can't possibly be important or relevant."

"I'm actually here to ask you about some of the history of Everlasting. I know your family goes back to the beginning, as does Sapphire's. I'm documenting some of the town's legends and stories of origin and thought you might have some historical documents that reference how Sapphire's ancestors brought magic to the town."

If Harriet's head could have spun around on her neck like *The Exorcist*, Zoe was certain it would have. Her entire face turned red and she began to sputter.

"That woman should be burned at the stake for her lies! My family is the source of the magic and she knows it. I have the proof if you're interested in seeing what a liar your aunt is."

"I, uh, yes. I would love to clear things up once and for all. I really want this document to be accurate."

"Then get in here and I'll show you."

Harriet let the door go and stalked across the living room muttering. Zoe caught the door before it closed and hurried after her. For an old broad, Harriet could move. She disappeared through a doorway at the back of the living room, and Zoe followed her through and into a surprisingly pleasant kitchen, given the surliness of the owner.

Harriet stood at a bookshelf along the back wall of a sitting room just off the kitchen, looking over a set of old leather-bound books. Finally, she located the one she was looking for and yanked it off the shelf and carried it into the kitchen, where she plopped it on the counter.

"Do you want to sit down?" Zoe asked, worried that the red coloring in Harriet's face hadn't yet subsided.

"Hell, no, I don't want to sit down. You're not going to be in my house long enough to warrant it."

Harriet opened the book and started flipping through the pages. Zoe leaned in to look and saw handwriting. It was a journal, and it looked old.

"Here." Harriet thrust the book at Zoe, pointing to a page. "Read that."

I MANAGED to slip the stone in my pocket when the pirates weren't looking. They threw the others overboard and I was certain I was next. I didn't know if I could survive the sea and make it to land, but I had to try. Not just to save myself but to make sure the emerald was not lost beneath the sea forever.

I swam for so long I lost consciousness. As I slipped into darkness, I remember my last thought was of my failure.

I awakened on the beach, unaware of how much time had passed. A few of my fellow travelers were there as well, the only survivors. Immediately, I checked my pocket, worried that the emerald had slipped out during my bitter struggle with the tumultuous water, and almost cried with relief when I felt it still in place. I knew then that we were meant to bring the stone here. That the magic it carried within was already working to create something special. Something found nowhere else on earth.

I couldn't risk keeping it with me. I had to hide it somewhere that no one would ever look. Where it could be safe forever, permeating the ground and bringing life into whatever it reached.

ZOE FLIPPED THE PAGE, but that was the last entry in the journal. "What happened after that?" she asked.

Harriet yanked the book from her and slammed it closed. "He died. But he succeeded in hiding the stone, and it's remained hidden all this time and will remain that way. The magic protects it."

"And it was a relative of yours who wrote the journal?"

"Of course. His name was Reginald Hatch."

Zoe frowned. Somewhere in the back of her mind was a distant memory of that name. Then it hit her.

"I've seen that name," Zoe said. "In Sapphire's family Bible. Hey, you two must be related."

Harriet's eyes widened and she clutched the kitchen counter as if she were going to pass out. "Get out. I won't hear those lies in my own house. You're just like your aunt. You can't admit the truth, even when it's right in your face."

Zoe didn't even bother to argue. There was no point and besides, Harriet didn't have anything else to show her. "Thank you for your time," she said, and headed out of the house.

She could feel the two guys painting staring at

her as she walked down the sidewalk and hurried away. One of them whistled, and she kept walking. A lady pulling weeds at the house next to Harriet's shook her head.

"I don't know why she hired those two hooligans," the woman said. "The Belmont brothers have never been anything but trouble."

Zoe forced herself not to turn around and look, because she knew they were staring right at her. Instead, she increased her pace and kept going, her gaze locked on the sidewalk in front of her. She could hear them laughing as she walked away.

They heard her identify herself to Harriet, so they knew she was Sapphire's niece. Was that why they'd whistled? To unnerve her? Because if so, it had worked. The brothers were creepy, and so were the whistling and the laughing. She wanted to put as much distance between herself them as quickly as possible.

DANE WAS CLEANING the grout bucket when Zoe pulled up, the engine of her econobox whining as it turned in the driveway, going way faster than was probably advisable. He rounded the corner in time to see her jump out of the car and hurry for the front door. Something was wrong. He knew that look and that walk, and neither was a good thing.

He rinsed off his hands and went in the back door and found her in the kitchen, strangling a bottle of water like it owed her money.

"Let me help you," he said as he took the water from her and removed the cap. He handed it back, and she took a big gulp.

"I promise I didn't step on the grout," she said. "I could tell it was fresh. I walked in between."

"The grout is fine," he said, "but you're not. What's wrong?"

"This thing happened and I got nervous, then mad at myself for being nervous, and...I don't know."

"Tell me."

She took another drink of water, then told him everything that had happened since she'd left that morning. When she got to the part about the Belmont brothers, he could feel anger coursing through him.

"They had no business messing with you like that," he said.

"I probably made it into something that it wasn't. I mean, it's not like men haven't whistled at me before. It's just that it felt creepy. You know, like I needed to rush away from there and rinse with bleach, then shower for a day or two."

"That's a pretty strong feeling. The woman I used to know always told me that feelings like that shouldn't be ignored because they might save your life."

"That woman was a pain in the ass."

"That's a whole other topic, but on this particular subject, I don't think she was wrong."

She stared at him for several seconds, then blew out a breath. "Fine. I was right. They're weird and probably dangerous, and it would probably be smart for women—not just me—to stay away from them. But I scurried away like a chicken and that pisses me off."

He smiled. "I bet it does."

"With everything that's going on, I just don't feel like myself."

He got the impression her worries went further than just the situation with Sapphire. "Is something else wrong?"

"Nothing you can help with. I got a call from my boss earlier. Things are heating up in LA."

"I assume this is about that promotion you want?"

"Yeah."

"I'm really sorry. I know how badly you want this."

She forced a smile. "It's all right. It's not like I'm out of a job or anything, just looking a bit sketchy on the promotion. I know people at other stations. I'll put out some feelers when I get back to LA.

There are some smaller markets that would appreciate my education and experience."

"Of course there are," he said. Dane didn't know anything about California news stations, but whatever was going on had Zoe miserable.

"Anyway, enough about that," Zoe said. "The important things are Mr. Simmons is allergic to cats and is in the throes of a reaction right now, the Belmont brothers are creepy and probably capable of anything, and there might have really been an emerald which may or may not have been hidden in Everlasting."

"But we still have no idea where it might be hidden, and Harriet probably has the only recorded reference to it."

"That ended abruptly because he died." Zoe sighed. "I don't suppose we could take out an ad in the local newspaper and say all that."

"To what end? Even if the thieves believed that Sapphire didn't have a map, the logical place for them to think the emerald is hidden is still the lighthouse."

"This sucks," she said. "I've completely lost my ability to think about this any longer. I'm going to go upstairs and make some notes so that I don't forget any of this, then I'm going take a shower until there's no more hot water. Maybe that will help clear my mind and erase the itchy feeling I got from the Belmont brothers."

"That's a good idea. I'm leaving in about half an hour but I'll lock up everything before I go."

"Are you still going to the Magic Eight Ball?"

He nodded. "I don't know that I can find out much, but I'll try to get some info on Simmons and the Belmont brothers. If Simmons is one of the guys, he's got a partner. Maybe I can get an idea of who that might be."

"I'll see you tomorrow then."

He hesitated, wanting to suggest he stay at the lighthouse that night, but one look at Zoe's body language and he knew she'd never go for it. She was too stressed, angry, upset, and tired to even entertain being closed up with him all night.

"Yep. First thing tomorrow. Call if you need anything and be sure to pull the dead bolts when you come back downstairs."

"I will. Thanks."

He nodded and headed out the back door to finish putting away his tools. He hoped he could find out something tonight that helped. Not that he was counting on it, but seeing Zoe so dejected made him ache for her. If he thought it would help, he'd fly to LA himself and punch someone out to get her that job. But that situation was completely out of his control. The one with Sapphire, however, he could help with.

He just had to figure out how.

ZOE STEPPED out of the shower and dried off, then wrapped a towel around her wet hair and headed into the bedroom for clothes. The steady stream of hot water had done wonders for her stiff body but unfortunately hadn't even put a dent in clearing up her confused mind. Sapphire, her job, her feelings for Dane, were all cobbled together in one big tangled mess. What she needed to do was focus, and since she couldn't focus on three things at once, and one of them was a distraction she didn't want to focus on at all, she needed to direct all of her attention to fixing things for Sapphire.

It wasn't as though she was out of a job and would be starving somewhere under a bridge. She could return to LA and step right back in the same job she'd had when she left. The only difference was, she'd be feeding all her educated findings to a bimbo instead of a douche. Not really a step up or down. Anyway, the whole job thing could wait until she was back in California.

The Dane thing could wait forever. That was territory she'd never planned to revisit when she left six years ago, and she couldn't see any reason to bring more aggravation and conflict into her life now. Realizing she still had feelings for him had been surprising and depressing but that didn't mean she had to change anything. Time would fix it all.

If she kept saying that, then she was certain it would happen.

She had pulled a T-shirt and sweats out of her suitcase before she went to shower but now that she was staring down at the garments, they didn't make sense. It wasn't as if she were going anywhere else tonight, and Dane should have been gone some time ago. Might as well put on her pajamas, go downstairs to pull the dead bolts, and feed the cats. Then she was going to crawl in bed and try to get some much-needed sleep. Even though the last time she'd gone to bed this early, she'd been eight years old.

The sheets were crisp and cool when she slid down in them and pulled the comforter up to her chin. She looked out the window at the moon, glowing up in the night sky, and drifted off.

Her cell phone startled her out of sleep and she bolted upright so quickly, she made herself dizzy. It took her a second to realize where she was and what had awakened her, and she grabbed her phone off the nightstand. She panicked when she saw Sapphire's name in the display.

"Sapphire?" she answered. "Is something wrong?"

"Is this Zoe Parker?" a male voice asked.

"Yes. Who is this? Where is Sapphire?"

"This is Dr. Williams. There's a situation with

your aunt. I need you to get to the hospital as soon as possible."

"What happened? Is she all right?"

"I'd rather explain when you get here."

"Okay. I'm on my way."

Chapter Ten

Zoe threw the phone on the bed and grabbed her jeans and a shirt from her suitcase and pulled them on. As she was tying her tennis shoes, she yelled for Cornelius. A second later, he popped through the wall of the bedroom, startling her all over again.

"Jesus, I wish you wouldn't do that," she said.

"But the door is closed," Cornelius said.

"Then yell ahead or something. One of these days, you're going to give me a heart attack and then where would we be?"

"That wouldn't be optimum." He looked at her and frowned. "Why are you getting dressed? It's 11:00 p.m."

"The hospital called. Something happened with Sapphire."

Cornelius's eyes widened. "What happened? Is she all right?"

"The doctor wouldn't say. I have to go to the hospital now. I'll call Dane on the way and let him know what's happening, but I need you to watch the lighthouse. If anyone tries anything, scare a cat at them and try to get a look at a face if possible. Remember anything they say."

"Of course. Please hurry. The sooner you get there and back, the sooner I'll know what's happening with Sapphire."

"I'll get there as fast as the econobox will manage."

She shoved her phone in her purse, grabbed her car keys, and ran to the rental car. As soon as she hit the highway, her foot slammed completely against the floorboard, but when the car hit seventy miles per hour, the engine refused to push it any further. What the hell? Now was not the time to run up against one of those stupid engine governors, but no matter how hard she stomped on the pedal, the vehicle refused to go any faster.

She was five miles down the road when she remembered to call Dane.

"Crap!" She dug her phone out of her purse and dialed Dane's number, then prayed he answered. On the fifth ring, she was about to give up hope when the call connected.

"Zoe?" he answered. "Is something wrong?"

She told him about the call from the hospital.

"I'll drive you," he said.

"I'm already on the highway. I meant to call sooner but I dashed out and then I was so busy thinking about what could be wrong and watching the road that I forgot. I need you to go to the lighthouse. If they're watching, then they saw me leave. They know it's empty. Are you at home?"

"No. I'm still at the bar, but I'm leaving right now. Concentrate on the road and don't worry about the lighthouse. And call as soon as you know something about Sapphire."

"I will."

She hung up the phone and banged on the steering wheel, cursing the stupid car for not going any faster. It would take Dane at least twenty minutes to get to the lighthouse from downtown, and she'd left almost ten minutes ago. If they were there, lurking somewhere nearby in the woods, that gave them a good thirty minutes to look around the lighthouse.

It wouldn't take them ten to find the notes she'd left on the desk in her aunt's room.

DANE JUMPED up from his chair, startling Monte and Sam and their glasses of whiskey.

"I've got to run." He tossed some bills on the table and hurried out of the bar without taking the time to explain. He could do that tomorrow when it was daylight and he was certain the lighthouse was secure.

Because of the festival traffic, his truck was parked two blocks over, so he took off running. When he sped around the corner on the street where he'd parked, he frowned. Something didn't look right. As he got closer, he realized his tires were flat. All four of them.

Cursing, he turned around and ran back to the bar and hurried over to Monte.

"I need to use your truck," he told Monte.

Monte and Sam glanced at each other, clearly confused but cluing in to the urgency.

"Sure," Monte said, and rose from his chair. "I'll settle up with Shorty later."

"I'm coming too," Sam said, not wanting to miss out on whatever was going on.

Dane hurried out of the bar and down the sidewalk, wishing Monte and Sam moved a little faster, but that was as futile as wishing his tires back to normal. The two old fishermen shuffled along at the fastest pace they could manage and were both huffing like freight trains by the time they reached Monte's house. Monte fiddled with his keys, trying to open the front door, and Dane struggled to control his impatience.

No way those tires went flat on their own. Someone had done it, and he was betting money that word had gotten back to the Belmont brothers that he was asking questions about them. It was just the kind of juvenile trick they'd play. He just hoped they'd only let the air out and that the tires weren't slashed. If they were, the trick would be juvenile *and* expensive.

They traveled through Monte's living room and kitchen. Monte grabbed the truck keys off a pegboard hanging next to the door that led into the garage, and they headed for the truck. Monte gave Dane the keys and he ran around to the driver's side. As he climbed inside, he realized Monte and Sam were getting in the passenger's side.

"What are you doing?" Dane asked.

"We're going with you," Monte said. "Something's wrong and we're going to help."

Dane didn't have time to argue and wasn't about to get in a scrap with two seniors, so he shoved the key into the ignition and turned.

Nothing happened.

He tried again. Still nothing.

"When was the last time you drove this truck?" Dane asked.

"I don't know," Monte said. "A month. Maybe two. When I went to the eye doctor."

"That was in June," Sam said.

Dane groaned. "Your battery is dead. How can you go four months without driving?"

"Social Security is direct deposit," Monte said.

"My bills are auto-drafted and the bar serves food. Doctors are the only thing I need to leave for."

"Sam?" Dane asked. "I don't suppose you have your car keys on you?"

Dane knew Sam usually caught a ride with Shorty at closing time. His house was a good four blocks away but if Dane could go without the slow twosome, he might be able to get to the lighthouse before tomorrow morning.

"Now don't go getting your panties in a bunch," Monte said. "I've got one of those jump-starters on the shelf there. It will only take a minute."

Monte's minute became a very long eight spent over missing cables and much discussion over the proper way to attach the starter. Finally, Dane all but pushed the two out of the way, and when the truck fired up they all climbed back inside. Dane backed out of the garage and took off down the street as fast as he dared given that festival people were still filtering down the streets to their cars.

"Hey," Monte said, "you never told us what the emergency is."

Dane glanced over at the two men and shook his head. All this running around and neither of them had bothered to ask that question until now. Their boredom level must be high for them to sign up for anything without question.

"I need to get to the lighthouse," he said, and explained the situation.

Monte and Sam exchanged worried looks.

"Did the doctor say what happened to Sapphire?" Sam asked.

"No," Dane replied. "Just that Zoe needed to get to the hospital as soon as possible."

"And all your tires are shot?" Monte asked.

Dane nodded. "Either someone let the air out or slashed them. I'm hoping it's the first."

The two fishermen exchanged looks again.

"What?" Dane asked. "You keep looking at each other like there's something I'm not saying. If you know anything about all of this, spill it."

"We don't know anything," Monte said, "or we'd have told you, but I saw that Hinkley boy head out of the bar right after you talked with Shorty. Were you asking him about the Belmont brothers?"

"Yes."

Monte nodded. "Then my guess is Hinkley tipped them off."

"I figured that might be the case," Dane said. "Why does that have you looking like you ate something bad?"

Monte glanced at Sam again, then looked back at Dane. "You don't think someone would hurt Sapphire just to get Zoe out of the lighthouse, do you?"

Dane clenched the steering wheel. No. He hadn't thought that was a possibility.

But he was thinking it now.

ZOE RUSHED into the hospital and Mary Jo looked up at her in surprise as Zoe ran up to the desk, out of breath.

"Where is Sapphire? Is she okay? What happened?" All of the questions came out at once.

Mary Jo rose from her chair and gave Zoe a concerned look. "Ms. Sapphire is fine. I just looked in on her a couple minutes ago. What is this about? You're panicked."

Zoe's stress level dropped by a thousand times, but her confusion shot right up to replace it. "I got a call from Dr. Williams. He said something had happened to Sapphire but he wouldn't talk about it over the phone. He said I needed to get here as quickly as possible."

Mary Jo's frowned. "Honey, there's no Dr. Williams on staff here."

What the hell?

"You're sure?" Zoe asked.

"Positive. I know every doctor who walks through those doors."

Zoe pulled out her cell phone and showed Mary Jo the call activity. "Look. That's a phone call from Sapphire's phone that she has in her room with her."

Mary Jo stared at the phone, her eyes widening. "I don't like this. Come with me."

Mary Jo headed for the hallway, and Zoe ran around the desk and through the door to join her. They hurried down the hall to Sapphire's room, and Mary Jo quietly pushed the door open and they walked inside. Sapphire lay on her bed, snoring lightly.

"Her vitals all look good," Mary Jo said. "Where is her cell phone?"

"It was on the tray with her Kindle when I left today."

"Well, it's not there now."

Zoe dialed Sapphire's number and a couple seconds later, they heard the phone signaling an incoming call. The sound was coming from the bed. Mary Jo lifted the covers and located the phone next to Sapphire's side. She pulled it out and handed it to Zoe, who checked the display.

"There's the outgoing call," Zoe said.

"And you're sure it wasn't Sapphire?"

"It was definitely a man's voice. Who is the doctor on call tonight?"

"Dr. West, but she's a woman and has a voice kinda like those singing cartoon chipmunks. I don't think she could sound like a man even if she tried."

Zoe motioned to the door and they went into the hallway.

"Is the front entrance the only way to access these rooms?" Zoe asked.

"No. There's employee access on the other side

of the building, but no one monitors it. We use key cards to get in."

"Can you find out who used their key card in the past couple hours? Someone made that call and I want to know who."

"I can ask security if they'll give me a log, but they'll probably ask for a supervisor's approval. Maybe we're overreacting. Maybe it was just a joke."

It was clear Mary Jo was grasping at straws, but Zoe didn't have time to make her feel better. The truth wasn't pretty, but it was what they had to deal with.

"Look," Zoe said, "I know Sapphire still doesn't remember what happened the night she fell, but I have reason to believe someone broke into the light-house and startled her. She dropped a flashlight and Mace when she fell."

Mary Jo looked stricken. "You don't think someone is trying to hurt Ms. Sapphire, do you?"

"I don't know what to think, but I don't like any of this."

"I'm calling the sheriff," Mary Jo said. "She's got all them fools just lounging around in tight pants. One of them can lounge outside your aunt's hospital room."

"You do that, but I have to get back to the lighthouse."

"Wait! The deputy will want to talk to you."

"Tell him to call me, or he can talk to me in person tomorrow. Something's not right. I've got to get back home."

Zoe rushed past the obviously distressed Mary Jo, but there was no time to explain what was going on, and Zoe was fairly certain she knew what that was. Someone had tricked her out of the lighthouse. Cornelius had seen two men. One of them could have made the call from Sapphire's phone while the other waited in the woods until she left.

She yanked her cell phone out of her pocket and dialed Dane's number as she ran to the car, praying that he'd made it to the lighthouse and that whoever was lurking there hadn't gotten the jump on him. At first, she'd been scared. Then she'd been confused and worried.

Now she was just mad.

Chapter Eleven

Cornelius was more stressed than he'd been that moment he first appeared at the lighthouse and found out he was dead. And that definitely ranked right up there as one of his all-time stressful moments. Zoe's car had barely disappeared down the drive when he heard rattling at the front door. Zoe couldn't pull the dead bolt from outside and Cornelius couldn't touch things, so the front door had been left vulnerable.

Cornelius popped outside and saw a man in black pants and shirt and wearing a black ski mask, working on the door lock. When his attempts were unsuccessful, he began cursing and Cornelius recognized his voice as that of the larger man the night Sapphire fell. Not exactly an earth-shattering revelation, as he'd assumed it was one of the two. Otherwise, it would mean an entire band of thieves was trying to get inside Sapphire's house to locate something that Zoe had told him no one was ever likely to find. And that was assuming it was even still in Everlasting.

He watched as the man took out a different set of tools and started on the lock again. This time he was successful. Cornelius heard a click and the man twisted the doorknob and pushed the door open. Cornelius hurried inside after the man, trying desperately to come up with a way to stop him. If only he could touch things. He could hit the man over the head and call 911. They'd send someone out even if there was no voice on the other end. But sadly, his limited skill set only left him the option of terrorizing cats. Unfortunately, the smaller man was the one who'd seemed to have a big fear of the animals.

Still, if cats were the only weapon he had, then by God, he was going to use them.

He watched as the man made his way through the living room, opening drawers on the various tables and shuffling through the documents. Then he inspected all the pictures on the walls, even taking them down and feeling the backs to make sure nothing was hidden inside. Cornelius scanned the room for a pair of glittering eyes, but all of the furry creatures appeared to have taken leave of the area.

Cornelius hurried into the laundry room, in case

one or more had fled that direction, but it was empty as well. When he came back into the living room, he saw the man disappearing up the stairs. Cornelius went up after him and watched as he entered Zoe's room. He started off by searching her suitcase, then moved on to the rest of the room. Cornelius looked everywhere—the closet, under the bed, behind the laundry basket—but there wasn't a cat in sight. It figured that the only time he needed to find one sitting on a toilet, they were all hidden from view.

The door to the storage room was closed so the only place left for the cats was Sapphire's room. Cornelius ran out of the bedroom and up the stairs, then had to stop halfway and catch his breath. Death was no fun at all. And really, if you were going to have all these restrictions—can't touch things, can't eat things, can't put on a pair of pants, can't leave a designated area—then it was only fair that you got handed a body that had Olympic conditioning. And just as soon as he had God's ear on the matter, he planned on telling him that.

Finally, he was able to drag in a breath without wheezing and took off up the stairs again, this time managing to make it all the way to the landing. He stopped at the threshold, not wanting to spook the animals before the timing was right, and peered inside. Sure enough, ten sets of glittering eyes twinkled at him from underneath furniture and behind curtains.

He eased into the room and took inventory of the location of everyone, trying to figure the best way to scare them all out of the door at the same time. As he edged near the desk, he saw Zoe's notes about the emerald right on top and on full display. More than ever, Cornelius wished he could touch things. It was paper. It was practically light as air, but when he reached for it, his hand passed right through the notebook and into the desk.

He couldn't let the intruder get into Sapphire's room. It would only take him seconds to locate Zoe's notes and be out the door with them. And Cornelius wouldn't have anything to tell Zoe because he still had no way to identify the man. He inched over behind the bed, trying not to spook the animals before he was ready, then stood in the corner and listened. The intruder was still moving around below him. He could hear the floorboards squeak in the guest room as he moved from side to side. Then the movement went farther away and Cornelius heard the sound of footsteps coming up the stairs.

He took in a deep breath, then started singing "Hound Dog" at the top of his lungs. Elvis Presley, he was not, but he had the cats screaming. Their response was instantaneous. They scrambled from their hiding places and ran one another over getting out the bedroom. Cornelius dashed for the landing, still singing, and arrived just in time to see the frantic cats race down the stairs, knocking the intruder off his feet.

The intruder fell backward and tumbled several steps down before crashing into the winding wall. Sleepy, the big Maine coon and slowest of the bunch, ran right across the intruder's head, his effort to flee not in the least bit impeded by the fallen man. Cornelius hurried down after him, hoping the fall had dislodged his mask, but was disappointed to see it still in place. The man pushed himself up and scanned the stairs, then turned as if he were going back upstairs.

As Cornelius started downstairs to attempt a reverse cat run, headlights flashed through the living room window and he heard an engine. It was too loud to be Zoe's car and it didn't sound like Dane's truck, either. It must be the intruder's partner!

Heavens, now there were two to contend with, and him trying to pull athletic moves in boxers and no shoes. This entire situation was out of control. The man on the stairs froze when he heard the engine and turned around to peer down the stairs. He cursed, then, in a move Cornelius wasn't expecting at all, ran down the stairs and out the back door, pausing long enough to lock it and pull it closed behind him.

At that moment, thunder boomed and lightning

lit up the sky. Seconds later, golf-ball-sized hail began to pelt down. The man let out a cry as a large piece of hail hit him on the forehead, then he threw his arm over his forehead and ran for the woods near the lighthouse. Cornelius watched his retreating figure and threw his hands in the air.

What in the world was going on?

The hail pounded against the side of the lighthouse, creating a repetitive droning sound that almost covered up everything else, but Cornelius still managed to hear faint cries. It sounded like they were coming from up front. Since the hail passed right through him, Cornelius didn't have the same issues as normal people—chalk one up for being a ghost—so he headed around front in time to see three men hurry in through the front door.

What now?

Cornelius headed inside, resigned to spending the rest of the night herding cats, and slid to a stop when he saw Dane and two other men standing in the living room. He stuck his head back outside and peered at the old truck in the driveway. It must belong to one of the men with Dane.

So the cavalry had arrived.

Now that he'd done all the work.

DANE POINTED to the living room and gave

instructions to Monte and Sam. "Check the windows. Make sure they're all secure. I'm going to check the back door."

He headed into the laundry room and checked the door and windows, but everything was secure. Back in the kitchen, Monte and Sam both nodded.

"Everything's locked up tight," Monte said. "The dead bolt wasn't drawn but maybe she forgot or hadn't closed things up for the night."

"Okay. Let's check upstairs. You two take the second floor and I'll take the third. Look in closets, under beds...wherever a man could hide. I have to be certain this place is clear before Zoe gets back."

They nodded and all headed up the stairs. Dane made quick work of Sapphire's bedroom and bathroom, pausing when he passed the desk. He picked up the notebook and scanned the notes. They were all about the emerald. Surely, if anyone had been inside, they'd have taken these notes with them.

He went back downstairs and met Monte and Sam on the second-floor landing, where they assured him that the storage room was clear and nothing was hiding in the guest room except angry cats.

"Darn thing took a swipe at me when I moved the curtains," Monte said and showed Dane the two spots on his hand with tiny droplets of blood. "Hissed so loud that at first I thought a snake had gotten me."

"You never know what Sapphire might be sharing her house with," Sam said.

"They're definitely spooked," Dane said, "but that could be because of the hail."

"And what the heck is that about?" Monte asked. "Between all this rushing about, that damned cat, and that hail pelting down on me, I'm going to be too sore to get out of bed tomorrow."

"You'll probably feel better when the bar opens," Sam said, and winked at Dane.

Dane frowned as the hail continued to pound against the lighthouse, thinking of Zoe in her economy rental. He pulled out his cell phone and dialed her number again, but just as it had before, the call went straight to voice mail. No way Zoe had intentionally turned off her phone. The only thing he could figure was that the storm was interfering with the signal. Hopefully, she'd be in touch soon.

He waved his hand at Monte and Sam, gesturing them downstairs. Dane opened the blinds on the front window and they all stared outside at the hail that bounced on the ground like rubber balls. The entire lawn was almost covered in white ice.

"Being on the water all those years," Sam said, "I've seen some strange weather, but this one beats all."

Monte nodded. "It's way too cool for hail. We should have been done with it months ago."

"Then where did it come from?" Sam asked. "I watched the weather report before I left for the bar. We're due rain tomorrow but otherwise, it was supposed to be clear."

"Says who?" Monte asked. "That idiot weatherman? He hasn't been right since Kennedy was president."

"Maybe even before," Sam said.

"I don't know where it came from," Monte said, "but I hope it stops while there's still something left of my truck."

"I'm really sorry about this," Dane said. "I'll pay to get it fixed."

"Heck no you won't," Monte said. "I've been paying that insurance company premiums for decades. They can send some money this way for a change."

"Then I'll cover your deductible," Dane said. "If it wasn't for me, the truck would be sitting inside your garage."

"I suppose that's fair," Monte said. "I don't suppose you'd want to cover the deductible for my roof repair? If this is coming down over in town, I'll probably need a new one."

"I think that one's on you," Dane said. "I hope Zoe isn't driving in this."

"She'd pull over if she got caught in it," Sam said. "Zoe's no fool."

Dane nodded, and it wasn't that he disagreed

with Sam. Zoe definitely wasn't a fool, but right now she was stressed and worried and probably scared for Sapphire and the lighthouse. All those emotions rolled up together didn't always lead to the most rational decision-making, even for otherwise logical people.

"Look!" Monte elbowed Dane. "Looks like headlights."

They all moved closer to the window, watching as the beams of light danced on the trees across the road. When the car swung into the driveway, the hail stopped as suddenly as it had begun. The complete quiet in the lighthouse was slightly spooky, and Dane wondered if Cornelius was lurking about somewhere.

"That's Zoe!" Dane said, and rushed outside.

Chapter Twelve

When she'd seen the strange truck in her driveway, a wave of fear washed through Zoe, but then she saw Dane exit the lighthouse and the fear was quickly replaced with relief. She jumped out of the car and hurried over to him.

"Are you all right?"

"Did anyone break in?"

"What happened with Sapphire?"

"Did they get my notes?"

They both fired off questions at once.

"Let's get inside before more weird weather blows through here," Dane said.

"Is that hail all over the lawn?" Zoe asked as they headed into the lighthouse. "That must be why I couldn't get a hold of you. I called several times but it went straight to voice mail."

"My calls did the same thing," Dane said.

Zoe stepped inside and drew up short when she saw Monte and Sam standing in the living room. Despite overwhelming confusion, good manners won out and she gave the fishermen a smile and moved forward to hug each of them. "It's good to see you," she said. "I wish it were under better circumstances."

"That can be arranged if you drop by the bar," Monte said. "Any night but Sunday, of course. We take that night off." He winked.

Zoe smiled. The bar was closed on Sunday or she was certain the two would be at their usual table just like every other night.

Sam jabbed Monte with his elbow. "Let's get out of here and leave these kids alone. It's past my bedtime and I've had more exercise tonight than I usually do all season."

"What? Oh, right," Monte said. "Do you need a ride home, Dane?"

"I can take him," Zoe said, still completely confused about what had happened at the light-house while she was gone. "It was nice seeing you again."

The two fishermen nodded and headed out. Dane closed the door behind them and looked back at Zoe, who had her hands on her hips.

"What the heck is going on?" she asked.

"First, tell me about Sapphire."

"She's fine," Zoe said, and told Dane what had

transpired at the hospital. By the time she was finished, the scowl on his face said it all.

"You could have been injured or worse driving to the hospital," he said.

"That probably would have been a bonus as far as the thieves were concerned, and don't think it didn't occur to me when I realized what had happened. Me in a bed next to Sapphire would free up the lighthouse at night. I gripped the steering wheel so hard on the way back my hands still ache. Your turn."

Dane told Zoe about his truck tires and enlisting help from Monte and Sam. If she weren't so stressed, she might have found the story amusing, but right now she felt more overwhelmed than anything else.

"But no one was here?" she asked. "You're sure?"

"All the doors and windows were locked."

Zoe grabbed his arm. "What about Cornelius? Where is he?"

"I can't help with that one, but you're right. I expected him to show up when you did."

"Cornelius!" she yelled. "Are you here? I need to talk to you. Cornelius!"

She waited, scanning the downstairs rooms for any sign of the ghost, but everything was quiet. Now worried, she started for the stairs but before she made it two steps, Cornelius ran through the front wall and into the living room, gasping for air.

"Are you all right?" she asked, rushing over to his side.

"Not really," Cornelius said. "I'm dead."

"You were already dead. Why are you out of breath? Never mind. Is something wrong? Did you see anything?"

Cornelius nodded. "The bigger man was here."

"At the lighthouse?" she asked.

"Inside the lighthouse," the ghost corrected.

"Oh God," Zoe said, and relayed that information to Dane.

"How did he get in?" Dane asked. "I checked everything."

"He picked the lock on the front door," Cornelius said. "He had a set of tools...long and skinny. It took him a bit but he got it open and started looking around."

"My notes!" Zoe exclaimed.

"He didn't get that far," Cornelius said. "I scared all the cats out of Sapphire's room and they knocked him down the stairs. Then Sleepy trampled his face. I'm sort of partial to Sleepy now."

"So am I," Zoe said.

"Then Dane and those other men showed up," Cornelius said, "and he took off out the back door and into the woods. I followed him around the perimeter as much as I could but I lost him at the road."

Dane had been practically on the verge of exploding during her exchange with the ghost, so Zoe filled him in.

"That's why the dead bolt wasn't drawn on the back door," Dane said. "Monte thought maybe you forgot but I wasn't convinced."

Dane opened the front door and started inspecting the lock. A minute later, he started cursing.

"I can see marks here," he said. "Cornelius is right. Damn it. I wasn't counting on a professional but the tools Cornelius described sound like those I've seen a locksmith use."

"They played us," she said. "They lured me out of the house and disabled your truck. If it weren't for Cornelius spooking the cats, he would have left with all my notes."

Dane nodded. She could tell he didn't want to admit how easily they'd been outmaneuvered, but there was no denying that's what had happened.

"What next?" Zoe asked.

Dane shook his head. "What do you mean?"

"I mean, how far will they go the next time? We know they were unsuccessful, so what's next? Are they going to break in, guns blazing, and demand a map that I don't have? Are they going to hurt Sapphire so that she can't leave the hospital?"

Dane's jaw clenched. "Sapphire needs protection."

"Mary Jo called the sheriff to get someone to guard Sapphire's room. Given the situation, I think I had the right to request it."

"Of course you did. I would have done the same thing."

"I got a text from her a couple minutes ago that a deputy is stationed outside her door. I guess I should call them myself about this."

"I don't know about that. Think about it—what proof do we have that someone was inside the lighthouse? Once again, the only witness is Cornelius. Nothing is out of place. Nothing shows signs of entry and those tiny scratches on the door hardware will be summarily dismissed as manufacturer defect, damage from the hardware store, or damage I did while installing them. I'm assuming he wore a mask and gloves again?"

Zoe looked over at Cornelius, who'd been silently listening to their exchange. The ghost nodded.

"Yes," Zoe confirmed.

"Then unless Sleepy scratched him hard enough to bleed through that ski mask, we don't have a shred more evidence now than we did the first time."

"Damn it. And he knows that."

"He's counting on that. Let's face it, the only

reason we know for certain what is happening here is because of Cornelius. He's the one thing the thief didn't and couldn't possibly account for. But there's only so much benefit to Cornelius's observations."

Zoe frowned. "It does give us an advantage, though."

"Sure, but one we can't use with law enforcement."

"Not that part. You said we wouldn't even know someone had been inside if it weren't for Cornelius."

"Right."

"That means the thief thinks we don't know. He thinks he got in and out clean. Think about it—he was in a rush to get out of here, but he stopped long enough to lock the back door. Why bother unless it was to hide evidence that he'd been inside?"

Dane's eyes widened. "I get you. But what about the call from the hospital? No one can deny it happened and I seriously doubt anyone is going to have the stones to call you a liar about the content of the exchange."

"No. But it could be passed off as a prank. Or they could suggest that in her weakened and drugged state, Sapphire made the call herself."

"Why the heck would she do that?"

"A bid for attention?"

He stared.

"You and I know that Sapphire would never,

ever attempt to get attention, especially like that, but other people have and would. And an older person creating drama isn't exactly an isolated thing, especially when they've been relegated to hospitals and nursing homes and the like."

He sighed. "So if we assume that the thief thinks we have no idea he was here, then from his standpoint, we haven't been tipped off either time."

"Right. So the question is, does he step up his game, thinking he's still got a window of doubt, or does he get smart and patient?"

"Either way, protecting Sapphire is our first priority. The sheriff will make sure she's covered tonight but what about tomorrow night?"

"Tomorrow night, she'll be here," Zoe reminded him.

"Crap. I'd forgotten. I don't suppose there's any way to keep her there longer?"

"Not without chaining her to the bed or killing her. She was threatening the doctor when I walked in today. Barring something catastrophic, she's leaving the hospital tomorrow."

Dane shook his head, clearly frustrated.

"They won't try anything with both of us here," Zoe said. "That would be beyond stupid."

"But you're not going to be here forever," Dane said. "And Sapphire alone is an easy target."

Zoe thought about the phone call she'd had earlier. With the way things had gone down at her job, she could be on a plane back to LA ten minutes from now and it wouldn't change things there.

"I'm not leaving until I'm sure Sapphire is safe," Zoe said.

"What about your job?"

"I only have one aunt."

He was silent for several seconds, then nodded. "I'm sorry. I know what your work means to you."

Zoe shrugged, trying not to let her mind wander to all the unpaid hours of work and seminars, workshops, and additional certifications she'd hustled for over the last six years. All of it likely a complete waste of time when all she'd really had to do was give up all her personal ethics and morals and sleep with some short, balding, ugly men to achieve her goals. What an absolute joke.

"There are other jobs," she said and sniffed, everything about her currently-falling-apart life rushing in at once. "Hey, the weatherman here isn't doing such a great job. Maybe that position will open up."

Finally, the dam broke. All the fear, aggravation, helplessness, and anger pushed her over the edge and the tears started to fall. Horrified, she looked down but she knew Dane had already seen. She felt his arms circle around her and the warmth of his body pressed against hers, giving her the comfort she so desperately needed. That single moment where you felt everything was all right before you broke apart and got to face the fact that nothing had really changed.

She leaned against him and let the tears fall. He was just being a friend—taking care of her as he would anyone else who lost the plot in front of him. It didn't mean anything. Finally, when the tears stopped and she managed a single deep breath without hitching, she took a tiny step back. He released her immediately, but she could see the concern in his expression.

"I'm sorry," she said. "I guess everything caught up with me."

"Do you want to talk about it?"

"No. Maybe. I don't know." She sank down onto the couch and rubbed her nose with her finger.

He took a seat next to her but didn't say a word. Maybe it was the fact that she'd known him most of her life and for a big part of it, had known him intimately, but Zoe felt a level of comfort telling Dane her worries that she'd never felt with anyone else. No other man had come close, and even her friendships with other women were more surface level than substance.

"I feel like a fool," she said.

"I know for certain that's not true. What's wrong?"

She took a deep breath and blew it out, then told him. Everything. All the extra hours she'd put in at work and on additional education. All the times she'd filled in at a moment's notice and had never had a fault in her work. All the acting classes and late nights studying the pros. All the hair, skin, and body maintenance so that she remained at LA standards. And finally, how all of it was wasted because she wouldn't sleep with trolls.

When she was finished, she looked over at Dane, unsure what to expect. He had every reason to gloat. He'd always thought going to California was a mistake and he hadn't hesitated to say so. But instead, his expression was a mixture of anger and sympathy.

"If those guys weren't on another coast," Dane said finally, "I swear…"

He didn't have to finish the sentence. She knew exactly what Dane would do if he got his hands on the executives, and she couldn't help but smile just a little. It felt good to have someone care enough about her to be outraged over her situation. Not that she would have sanctioned what Dane had in mind. She would have gone out of her way to prevent it, but not because she cared about any of those awful men. Simply because the trolls weren't worth Dane going to jail over.

And they weren't worth her shedding another tear, either.

She rose from the couch and glanced around for Cornelius, but apparently, things had gotten too personal and the ghost had politely bowed out. She had to give him credit. For an entity that couldn't be forced to behave, Cornelius attempted to maintain a high level of manners. The walking through walls still startled her, but she was certain that wasn't his goal.

Dane rose as well and studied her. "Are you all right?"

"Actually, I feel better than I have in a long time. I mean, I'm still panicked over this whole emerald thing and Sapphire coming home in the middle of it, but the rest of it simply doesn't matter anymore. Now, one hundred percent of my energy can be devoted to getting Sapphire's life back to normal."

"You mean normal for Sapphire."

She smiled. "Yeah. Thank you for listening. I don't have people I can talk to that understand things the way you do."

"That's because they don't understand you the way I do."

He stepped closer until he was right in front of her, maybe an inch separating their bodies. Zoe knew he was going to kiss her and she knew she should stop him but at that moment, her heart completely overrode her mind.

He pressed his lips to hers softly at first, and the gentleness of his lips on hers sent her back to a past where everything was perfect. When simply being in his arms made all other hardships feel like small things that were easily overcome.

She wrapped her arms around him, enjoying the familiar feel of his muscular back. With physical activity being a primary component of his work, he'd always been in spectacular shape, and if anything, construction had improved on an already splendid product. He pulled her in close, pressing his body against hers, and deepened the kiss. She groaned, and the warmth swept through her body and the familiar feel of his lips and hands on her sent her back in time.

And suddenly, her mind jolted her back into the current date and time, and she broke away from him. This was a mistake and a distraction that neither of them could afford.

"I'm sorry," she said. "I just can't."

"I understand," he said. "It won't happen again."

"I'll give you a ride home."

"No. I can walk. It's not that far."

"It's forty degrees out there and windy."

"The cold air will do me good. I'll see you tomorrow morning."

He was out the door before she could respond. She stood there for several seconds, then hurried to the door to make sure it was locked. She checked the back door, even though she knew Dane had already gone through the same steps, then she hurried upstairs to her bedroom to change clothes, certain that sleep, if it happened, was going to be hard won.

Minutes later, she was warming up in her fuzzy pajamas and buried deep under the comforter. Cornelius had never reappeared, but somehow, she knew he was around and watching. If the thieves returned, he'd let her know.

Dane's kiss has scared her. It had awakened feelings she'd thought were long gone, and what troubled her even more was that the intensity hadn't waned. If anything, the pull to him was stronger than ever. She'd convinced herself she was over him...had dated other men, although she'd admit that none of those relationships had lasted very long or been of any substance. But she just told herself that's because she hadn't found the right one. That when the guy for her came along, everything would click, and it would be as though they were manufactured to fit together.

Like her and Dane.

She shook her head. That was a thought she could not entertain. Her future wasn't in Everlasting, and Dane's life would always be here. And as much as she considered herself a modern-day woman, a fling just wasn't something she could manage. Especially a fling with Dane. There were too many unresolved feelings. She'd managed to fool herself about them all these years, but now she had to face the truth.

She was still in love with him.

Unfortunately, their lives didn't mesh any better today than they had six years ago.

DANE SHOVED his hands in his pockets as he walked, cursing himself with every step. What had he been thinking? Scratch that. He was certain what he'd been thinking, and it fell under things he needed to turn a blind eye to. Like Zoe standing there looking so incredibly beautiful and so completely vulnerable. He could see how scared and exhausted she was and knew she needed his help.

Instead, he'd taken advantage of the situation and kissed her.

He shook his head. No. That wasn't completely fair. The last thing on his mind when he'd kissed her was that he was taking advantage, but he could see how it might look that way now. The reality was, he'd kissed her because he couldn't keep himself from doing it any longer. Since the first moment he'd laid eyes on her in Sapphire's kitchen, standing there in her rumpled clothes and clutching the oar like a baseball bat, he'd wanted to do exactly what he'd just done—pull her in close to him and kiss her senseless.

He'd managed to keep those feelings at bay. Until tonight.

And things had turned out so well. He cursed again. Zoe had so many things on her mind right now. So many critical things to stress over and figure out a solution for, and he'd thrown in another curveball, as if she weren't juggling enough already. In fairness, he'd already decided he was going to make a move before she left...leave her something to consider once again. But he'd jumped the gun.

Now Zoe was stressed and scared and would probably hesitate before asking him for help. That was the last thing he wanted. A conversation about their relationship—such as it was—wasn't something Dane was interested in having, especially now. But he didn't have a choice. Zoe needed to know that she could depend on him without any strings attached. He didn't even want her to pause before dialing his number on her phone.

So he'd apologize once more tomorrow and reassure her that it wouldn't happen again.

And then he'd make a liar out of himself and tell her how he really felt before she left.

Chapter Thirteen

Zoe sprang upright the next morning, glancing around for the source of the noise that had awakened her. Sleepy meowed at her from the nightstand and she realized the clock was missing, probably currently residing on the floor.

She reached over and rubbed him behind the ears. "You're lucky you've got brownie points with me. Good job, running over the bad guy's face."

Her eyes widened and she sucked in a breath. She'd been so overwhelmed with everything last night that it didn't even occur to her that Sleepy's somewhat violent bolt down the stairs and the hailstorm might help them identify the culprit. The hail she'd seen on the lawn had been large enough that it might cause bruises, and if Sleepy's claws had penetrated the mask, the guilty party might be sporting some scratches across his face.

It wasn't a sure thing, but it was a place to start.

She flung the covers back, startling Sleepy, who bolted off the nightstand and ran out of the room, then she headed into the bathroom for a quick refresh. Twenty minutes later, she was clad in jeans, tee, hoodie, and tennis shoes and ready to face what was certain to be a confused Sapphire. Zoe could only imagine the small riot that had ensued when her aunt had awakened and found a deputy guarding her door.

Even though it was barely seven thirty when she went downstairs, Dane's saw was already working out back. Zoe knew she had to speak to him, but for the life of her, she had no idea what to say. Even worse, she was afraid if she opened her mouth to say anything at all that she might end up admitting how she felt, and since she had no idea how she was going to deal with those feelings, there was no way she was letting that cat out of the bag. There were enough cats out of the bag at the lighthouse already.

Drawing in a breath and forcing herself to remain calm, she headed out the back door and waited until Dane finished cutting the piece of tile he was working with and turned. He drew up short when he saw her standing there, and she could see him stiffen as his eyes darted away from her, then back. A bit of relief passed through her. He was uncomfortable as well.

Thank God. If he'd stood there facing her, in all his cocky glory, she probably would have crumbled. This mature, cautious Dane was someone new. She felt as if she knew him but didn't.

"You're at it early," she said, then suddenly remembered his truck. "Oh no! You had to walk over here this morning. I am so sorry. I should have just told you to take my car."

"I didn't walk. I rode my motorcycle."

"But it's too cold to be exposed like that."

"I have a leather jacket and full face helmet. It's not bad. Unless I'm hauling tools or there's rain in the forecast, I usually ride it to jobs when I can. Winter will be here in full force soon enough and she'll be up for the season. I'm trying to squeeze those last few days out of her."

She should have known he'd have a bike. He always had. It had been a major point of contention between her and her dad, who'd raised hell about Zoe riding on it even with a jacket and helmet. Zoe had understood her dad's concern, but had completely ignored his rule about not getting on the bike. The truth was, she'd found racing along in the elements kind of thrilling, though she'd never let her dad hear her say that. He'd have had a small nervous breakdown.

"What are you going to do about the truck?" she asked. "Do you need a ride into town? I'm going there now to get some Danish from the bakery for Sapphire's breakfast."

"I appreciate it but I've already left a message for Henry, my mechanic, and asked him to go take a look for me. Hopefully, they just need some air. If I need new tires, then I'll have to come up with plan B until they can get them ordered and here."

"Okay, well, I'm headed out then."

As she started to turn to go, he said, "Wait."

She stopped and looked at him and he ran one hand through his hair.

"Look, Zoe, I want to apologize again for last night. I'm not going to lie and say I'm sorry I kissed you because I'm not. I wanted to and I did. But I should have taken your feelings into account and I didn't. You've got enough to worry about, and I don't need you wondering if you can count on me or if I have an ulterior motive. I want to assure you that's not the case. My immediate concern is making sure Sapphire is safe in her home, and I don't want you dealing with this alone."

All of the anxiety she'd felt over facing Dane that morning was swept away. "I'm really grateful for your help. There's no one else I would trust with this. And I would never think you had an ulterior motive. That's not the kind of man you are. I know some things have changed since I've been gone, but I doubt that's one of them."

His relief was obvious and instant. "Thank you for understanding."

"I understand a lot better than you think. And I kissed *you* because I wanted to."

Before she got herself into a conversation she wasn't ready for, she turned and walked back into the lighthouse. This time, he didn't stop her.

The entire drive to the hospital, she tried to focus her thoughts on what to do about the thieves and how to make Sapphire safe, but everything came back to that silly emerald. Unless they found the stone and it was secured away in a museum somewhere or they could prove it was long gone from Everlasting, Zoe was afraid the thieves wouldn't stop. And that simply wasn't an option.

When she walked into the hospital, Zoe was surprised to see Mary Jo behind the front desk. "Don't you ever get to go home?" she asked.

Mary Jo smiled. "I was waiting for you, actually."

"Is something wrong?" Zoe yanked her phone out of her purse and checked the display. "Did you call?"

"Nothing's wrong. Well, nothing major. I just wanted to warn you that Sapphire is more than a little testy. She got up this morning and decided she was going to do laps up and down the hallway. Of course, the first thing she saw when she walked out the door was Deputy September sleeping in a chair across from her room. I did my best to calm her down, but she was more than a little upset that we didn't wake her last night and let her know what was going on."

Zoe groaned. She'd been hoping to get back to the hospital and intercept the deputy before her aunt found out about the night's events. "I'm so sorry," Zoe said. "Thank you so much for waiting on me, but please go home and get some rest. You've got to be exhausted."

"I fully intend to, but I'm afraid that's not all. Ms. Sapphire pitched such a fit that one of the other nurses called Dr. Stephenson in. Well, she gave him a piece of her mind in a way that my granny back in Abilene would have been proud of and that might have gotten her arrested in more civilized places. Anyway, Dr. Stephenson called Dr. Prescott and he said if her vitals were fine to go ahead and release her."

Mary Jo pointed at the bag of Danish. "So I'm afraid that's going to be a to-go order and it comes with a disgruntled aunt."

Zoe froze. "She's being released now? As in I've got to spend the next thirty minutes in the car with her?"

"I'm afraid so." Mary Jo gave her a sympathetic look. "And I don't mean to pile more on you, but Deputy September is insisting on taking your statement before you leave with Ms. Sapphire."

"This day just keeps getting better. Thank you again, for holding all this together. I seriously owe you."

Mary Jo waved her hand in dismissal. "I love Ms. Sapphire and I took to you the first night I met you. I'm happy to help what little I can. If you or Ms. Sapphire have any worries about her injuries after you get her home, you can always call me. Dr. Prescott is always available to his patients by phone, but Ms. Sapphire might not be too anxious to let him know if there's a problem. I can usually pave the way for the doctors with some of their more, um, challenging clientele."

"The state of Texas lost big-time when you moved to Maine."

Mary Jo beamed. "That's just the nicest thing anyone's said to me all week. Good luck with this and remember, I'm only a phone call away."

Zoe nodded and headed for Sapphire's room just in time to hear raised voices coming from inside. She walked in and found the month of September facing Sapphire in a standoff. Zoe took one look at the two of them and immediately placed her bet on her old aunt.

"Everyone calm down," Zoe said.

They both turned to look at her and Sapphire scowled. "Well, it's about time you showed up."

"It's just past 8:00 a.m.," Zoe said, feeling sorry for her aunt's aggravation but not about to let

Sapphire push her around. "That's a decent hour for normal people, especially when I was up half the night."

Sapphire raised her eyebrows but didn't say another word, clearly cluing in that Zoe was not in the mood to cater to anyone else's drama.

"What can I help you with, Deputy?" Zoe asked.

"I need to take a statement about what happened last night from Sapphire," he said. "But she's refusing to cooperate."

Sapphire threw her hands in the air. "I'm not refusing anything. I've told him a million times that nothing happened. I took my meds and went to sleep and woke up this morning with him snoring outside of my room. That's my statement."

"She's right," Zoe said. "My aunt never awakened last night while I was here."

"So she called you in her sleep?" September asked.

Zoe held in a sigh. "It was a man's voice, and since I know my aunt's voice, I can assure you it was not her. Someone used her phone."

September didn't look convinced. "I just can't think of a reason someone would do that. I mean, if it's a prank, it's not a very funny one."

"I totally agree," Zoe said. "But Mary Jo told you exactly what happened, so you know what to put down for my statement. I don't have anything else to add. It was an alarming situation and not in the least bit funny."

"I suppose I could see if someone's kids were on the floor that late..." His voice trailed off. The deputy was at a complete loss. Zoe was fairly certain that the only way September would find the man who called her the night before was if he were standing in front of them and admitting to doing so.

"We appreciate any assistance you can provide us," Zoe said, "and thank you for watching my aunt's room last night. I wouldn't have been able to sleep without knowing you were here."

He looked slightly mollified and a little pleased. "I was just doing my job."

"Well, if that's all," Zoe said, "then I'm going to collect my aunt and take her home."

September nodded and Sapphire grabbed her bag of personal items and practically ran out of the room. Zoe hurried behind her as she blew past the nurse's station and out the front door.

"Don't you have to check out or something?" Zoe asked.

"Which one is your car?" Sapphire asked, scanning the parking lot.

"The white one over there," Zoe said. "Discharge papers? Nothing like that?"

"Mary Jo took care of it," Sapphire said.

Zoe made a mental note to get a gift basket for Mary Jo before she left Everlasting. Something with sweets, bath salts, and wine. The nurse had earned it ten times over.

Sapphire jumped into the passenger seat, threw on her seat belt, and looked at Zoe with all the impatience of a six-year-old on her way to Disney World. She waited until Zoe started the car to begin firing off questions.

"What the hell is going on? Who called you? Did anything happen at the lighthouse?"

Zoe explained everything that happened the night before to her aunt, leaving out, of course, the part about kissing Dane. Sapphire surprised her by listening without interruption, then sitting quietly for several seconds when she was done. Finally, her aunt shook her head.

"I don't know what to do," Sapphire said. "The entire thing is so ridiculous."

Zoe looked over at her aunt. "I thought you believed in the whole magic emerald thing."

Sapphire gave her a disapproving look. "It's not a 'thing' and of course I believe the legend. What's ridiculous is that anyone thinks I have information that leads to the location of the stone but haven't retrieved it myself."

"But you said if the stone was removed, the magic might leave Everlasting."

"If I knew where the stone was, I would simply ensure that no one else could find it."

"Seems like someone already did that since it

hasn't surfaced after all these years. Plenty of treasure hunting and construction has gone on in Everlasting since it was first established. I think we would have heard if anyone had unearthed a giant emerald."

"Yes, that does make it more interesting."

"I'm not sure 'interesting' is the word I'd use to describe this. 'Worrisome' is better but not strong enough. The reality is, as long as someone thinks you hold the key to finding the stone, you're not safe. The lighthouse isn't safe. They've tried twice already. The first time you fell and the second time they made me believe you had relapsed, just to get us out of the way. What if they up their game next time to actual injury?"

Zoe studied her aunt's face, and although she could tell Sapphire was struggling for the serene outlook she preferred to live by, her eyes gave away the worry she felt.

"What should we do?" Sapphire asked.

Zoe clenched the steering wheel and shook her head.

She didn't have an answer.

Chapter Fourteen

The welcoming committee was sitting at attention when Sapphire entered the lighthouse. Zoe had no idea how they knew Sapphire was coming as her aunt hadn't made a single noise walking from the car to the house, but they were all waiting expectantly when the front door opened. As soon as Sapphire entered, they crowded around her, meowing and shoving one another around, trying to rub her aunt's legs.

"Oh, my precious babies," Sapphire said, and bent over to give each of them a scratch on the ear. She gave Sleepy additional time and praised him for running over the intruder's face. Then she thanked all of them for helping Cornelius and apologized if they'd been startled by the ghost, assuring them that he was just trying to take care of their home.

Zoe skirted the cat frenzy and headed into the kitchen, where Dane was measuring a shiny new stainless steel range cooktop. He looked up at her as she walked around the island.

"They've been sitting like that for the last ten minutes," he said. "Usually they want to be as far away from the racket as possible, but not even me grinding down some of the edges on the cabinets seemed to faze them."

"I don't even want to speculate," Zoe said.

Dane nodded his understanding. Speculating on what was at play put them right back into the netherworld of Everlasting, and they already had more otherworldly things to process than either of them wanted.

Finally, Sapphire finished making the rounds and walked into the kitchen to give Dane a hug and kiss on the cheek. Then she took a good look at the room for the first time since she'd walked inside. Her eyes widened.

"Oh!" Both her hands came up to touch her cheeks. "Dane, this is simply gorgeous. The light green on the cabinets and the glass door fronts…I can't wait to see it with those countertops and the backsplash."

Dane smiled and Zoe could tell he was happy that she was pleased with his work. "Give me an hour and those countertops will be in. I'm measuring for the cutouts now. The edges are already done. I'll need another couple days for the backsplash, though."

"You know I always tell you I'm not in a rush," Sapphire said, "and that's true, but I will say I can't wait to see it all done. Every room you remodel I think is the best one, but I'm going to go ahead and say it now, the kitchen is definitely my favorite."

"I'm glad you like it," he said.

"Like it? I love it. If my bedroom weren't so lovely, I might just sleep in it."

"I don't think it's fit for sleeping," Dane said, "but in a couple days you'll be back to baking everyone's waistline up another size."

"Yes, well, I guess that depends on if I'm around in a couple days, doesn't it?" Sapphire asked. "Zoe seems to have some concerns about my safety, and as much as I'd love to dismiss her as being ridiculously dramatic and overprotective, I'm afraid that would be foolish. I'm an optimist, but not a fool."

Dane sobered and nodded. "The situation is serious. You could have been hurt that first night and Zoe could have been last night, driving to the hospital like Mario Andretti."

"It was more like Fred Flintstone," Zoe said. "Given the top-end speed limit on the car, I was about to stick my feet out the door and push."

"Both were uncalled for," Sapphire said, "and

potentially dangerous. So we all agree that something has to be done."

"Yes," Dane said, "but the big question is what?"

"That's easy," Sapphire said. "First, we set a trap and catch the thieves."

Zoe looked over at Dane, wondering which one of them was going to point out the obvious flaws in her aunt's logic. When he remained silent, Zoe figured he'd decided that as a blood relative, it was Zoe's responsibility to call her aunt crazy.

"I think that might be difficult," Zoe said. "The thieves are probably waiting for me to leave before they return. It's easier with a lone target."

"So we'll make everyone think we left," Sapphire said. "Then we'll catch them in the act."

Zoe looked over at Dane for help, but he was still staring at Sapphire, his expression a mixture of uncertainty and contemplation, which was potentially scarier than Sapphire suggesting such a plan in the first place.

"Okay," Zoe said, "we are not qualified to pull off a sting. And despite the fact that we have an old ghost hanging around, this is not an episode of *Scooby-Doo*."

"Well of course we aren't," Sapphire said. "I have an army of cats. Not one silly dog."

"I think she's onto something," Dane said.

"You're serious?" Zoe stared at him in dismay.

"Why not?" he asked. "You and Sapphire can put out word that you're going to visit someone overnight or whatever, then head out of town and hole up in a motel. I'll leave at my usual time, then sneak back over after dark and wait for the thieves to show up."

Sapphire shook her head. "No way. You're not doing it alone. Either we're all in it or none of us are. There's two of them. You need all of us working together on this."

Zoe opened her mouth to launch another protest, then paused. Was it really as horrible an idea as it originally sounded? Cornelius had never seen the thieves carrying a gun, and they'd fled after Sapphire fell, so violence probably wasn't one of their primary objectives. If they thought the house was empty, they wouldn't come armed for battle.

Sapphire put her hand on Zoe's arm. "Honey, it's going to happen eventually. This way, we're controlling the time and we're ready for them."

Damn it! Zoe knew her aunt was right but she didn't like admitting it. Until the thieves were caught, every night Sapphire spent in the lighthouse she'd be jumping at every creak, just waiting for them to strike again. Short of getting her armed guards, setting a trap was the fastest way to resolve the situation and get Sapphire's life back to normal.

"Okay," Zoe said finally, "but you are to remain out of sight and ready to call the cops. This is not the time for you to test some Bruce Lee move or whatever else you've taken up lately."

"I start MMA classes next month," Sapphire said. "It's a shame they didn't offer them sooner."

"Yeah, that is a shame," Zoe said. "So what's the next step? You said earlier that 'first' we needed to set a trap and catch the thieves."

"Oh, then we find the emerald and make sure it's secure," Sapphire said.

Zoe blinked. "Just like that. We're going to find the emerald even though we have no clue as to its hiding place."

"I didn't say it would be easy," Sapphire said, "but it should be fun."

"First things first," Dane said, interrupting Sapphire's personal *Lord of the Rings* quest. "We need a plan for tonight."

"You want to do it tonight?" Zoe asked.

"Why wait?" he asked.

He was right, of course. There was no reason to wait until tomorrow night or the next night or the following week. All that did was give the thieves an opportunity to get the jump on them.

"Great!" Sapphire clapped. "Then let's head into the living room and start planning our coup."

And so they began.

Given that she worked for a news station, Zoe

had been to her share of war room meetings, but the one she was in now took the prize for the strangest collection of participants ever. Zoe and Dane sat on the couch and Sapphire was seated in her recliner. Cornelius, who'd attempted sitting in a chair but kept falling through, had finally given up and stood near Sapphire. But it wasn't the ghost that tipped the hand all the way to weird. It was the ten cats sitting in a row on the coffee table, quietly awaiting word from their leader.

Zoe looked down at her laptop where she'd been taking notes. "This is what we have so far. Sapphire will call everyone she knows and let them know that I'm taking her to Portland overnight for a girls' spa adventure to celebrate her hospital release. We will also go downtown where Sapphire will stop in on everyone she knows and provide them the same story."

Sapphire nodded. "That should get word around to everyone in town."

"Even the dead," Cornelius said, and laughed. "Sometimes I kill myself. Oh, look, I did it again."

Zoe gave him the side-eye and kept going. "What we need to figure out now is how Sapphire and I get back here without anyone knowing."

"I have an idea on that," Dane said, "but we're going to have to enlist some help."

"Who can we trust?" Zoe asked, and put her hand up to stop Sapphire before she started listing everyone she knew. "Who can *you* trust?" she asked Dane.

"Sam and Monte," Dane said. "They already know some of what's going on and they're pissed that someone's harassing Sapphire."

Zoe nodded. "And we know for certain they aren't involved since they were sitting in the bar with you when everything when down. Not that they were ever suspects, but it doesn't hurt."

"Agreed," he said. "So this is what we'll do. You and Sapphire will leave downtown and go to the Eastbound Motel just outside of town. The motel should have quite a few festivalgoers registered, so your car will be easy to hide in the mix. I'll have Monte and Sam pick you up and bring you back here."

"But both of them drive single-cab trucks," Zoe said. "And they can't exactly pull up in the driveway and let us out. For all we know, one of them could be watching from the woods like he was before."

"I have an idea about that," Dane said.

"What idea?" Zoe asked.

"Don't worry about it. Just get to the motel and I'll have it all worked out."

Zoe wasn't completely comfortable with that. Not because she didn't trust Dane but because she'd always been one of those people who had to know things. Asking her to remain in the dark was like asking her to not watch the weather report. She'd try to suck it up, but she figured she'd be asking for details before they ever arrived at the motel.

"Then that puts us back here midafternoon," Zoe said, "which gives Sapphire time to get some rest." She narrowed her eyes at her aunt. "No arguments. You just walked out of the hospital today."

"I am happy to take a nap along with my pretties," Sapphire said.

"Not just rest," Dane said. "You'll have to stay out of sight, which means upstairs. If I close the blinds downstairs, it might look odd given that I never have until I'm done for the day. Plus, since the new lighting hasn't been installed yet, the sunlight really helps as far as my work goes."

Zoe nodded. "We'll stay in our bedrooms and away from the windows. So what about tonight? I mean, specifically when they get here?"

"I want Cornelius patrolling outside," Dane said. "That way, he can warn us when they're here and we can get in position. My guess is they'll come through the front door since he was able to jimmy that one the last time and will assume you leave that way so the dead bolt won't be drawn. I'll hide behind the cabinet on the front wall in the living room. I want you guys upstairs. We'll move the refrigerator to block the back door so they can't get out that way. When they make it into the middle of the living room, I want Cornelius to yell so Zoe will know to come down the stairs. I'll leave my position to block the front door. Between us and the refrigerator, we'll have all exits blocked unless they want to jump through a window. Is Cornelius okay with all that?"

Zoe looked up at the ghost, who nodded.

"Yes, of course," Cornelius said. "Whatever it takes. Perimeter patrol, cat herding, I'm up for it."

Several of the cats hissed and Sapphire reached over to pet them. "He's just trying to help. He doesn't mean to startle you."

"No," Cornelius said. "I definitely meant to startle them."

The cats, in movement that seemed synchronized, all glared at Cornelius, then proceeded to lick their butts.

"That's not polite at all," Sapphire said, giving them a disapproving look.

"So when confronted, you think the thieves are going to stop and confess?" Zoe asked. "Promise not to do it again?"

Dane shook his head and looked over at Sapphire. "I know you're not a fan of guns but I'm going to bring two of my hunting rifles. We'll keep the thieves in place until the police arrive. That's why I want you out of sight and handy with your cell phone." He glanced over at the butt-cleaning cats. "Also, if things go wrong, maybe you can convince your friends to create havoc."

Sapphire frowned. "Breaking into my home,

putting my niece in a dangerous situation on the highway, forcing Cornelius to terrorize my babies… if you're willing to load up a shotgun with rock salt, I'll shoot them myself."

Zoe smiled. "Then looks like we're set."

Chapter Fifteen

By the time they left downtown, Zoe was convinced they'd spoken to half of Everlasting. If there was someone in the town who didn't know about their spa plans then they were deaf or living under a rock. Either way, they weren't a threat. They headed for Zoe's car with a sizable bag of baked goods that Sapphire had insisted on since she couldn't bake at her house, and Zoe set off for the highway.

It was only a ten-minute drive to the motel and Dane had been right about the parking lot. It was at least half full, and Zoe had no problem finding a space at the back of the lot where her car couldn't be seen by anyone driving by. As she cut off the engine, her cell phone signaled a text. It was from Dane.

Monte and Sam on way now.

"They'll be here soon," Zoe said. "He never did tell me what he'd cooked up."

"I hope it doesn't involve Monte's boat. He's horrible at cleaning. You can smell the thing a mile away."

"Well, if it does, we'll have all afternoon to shower."

"The cats would probably love it."

Zoe nodded, the question that had been hovering in her mind finally making its way out. "You really can talk to them, can't you? I mean, I've seen well-trained animals—my news station did a special on performance animals a couple months ago—but your relationship with the cats is a whole different thing."

"Communication with them is my gift. I'll admit that it's a bit odd and unfortunately, plays into that whole crazy cat lady thing, but we don't get to pick our magic."

Zoe had refused to believe Sapphire when she'd claimed an unearthly affinity for chatting with the cats, although Zoe would have been the first to say that her aunt was gifted at training them. But in the past six years, Sapphire had seriously upped her game, especially with that whole toilet training thing.

Cornelius had forced Zoe to reexamine her narrow views. Or perhaps normal views was a better way to put it. Being face-to-face with a real talking ghost tended to make one reconsider a lot of things. Now she was reassessing every absurd claim she'd ever heard an Everlasting resident make and wondering how many were true, even partially so.

"Can they talk back?" Zoe asked. "I mean, I know they talk but do you understand what they're saying?"

"Not in the way that I understand you. There are no words, but I feel their emotions and it allows me to understand what they're trying to communicate."

"But they understand your words."

Sapphire nodded. "I think at one time, I probably had an ancestor who could understand their language. Maybe the gift decreases as it passes on from generation to generation or maybe the gift is altered by the person it inhabits. Our biology is all the same but all different, so that would make sense. After all, aspirin can react different ways in different people."

"That's an interesting thought. You've never found anything in the journals about an ancestor who had an affinity for animals?"

"Unfortunately, no. It was the first thing I searched the journals for, hoping to find ways to increase my own skill. I thought perhaps the innate ability could be honed, bettered, if I had instruction, and perhaps that's the way it used to be also.

Back when people believed and weren't so dismissive."

Guilt coursed through Zoe. She'd never been dismissive of her aunt's beliefs but she'd humored her, and that was just as condescending.

"I'm sorry I never really believed you," Zoe said.

Sapphire squeezed her hand. "Please don't apologize for wanting to be a normal person with normal family. Very few believe. In Everlasting, the percentage of the population that believe in or have gifts themselves is much higher than normal, but the disbelievers are growing every day."

"Probably because with every generation we get more jaded and convinced we know better. Like me."

Sapphire smiled. "You're not nearly as bad as some. But you definitely got your father's stubborn streak."

"Does he have an ability?" Zoe asked.

"I don't think so. I've watched all these years, of course, in case his gift was latent and was going to show up later in life. Mine didn't until I was twenty-eight."

"Really? So you were my age?"

Sapphire was silent for several seconds. "The gift tends to act the same way along bloodlines. The journals contain few references to gifts but they were mostly written by men. The ones that were written by women all hint to changes that happened but not until they were approaching thirty years old."

Sapphire's tone changed as she talked, growing more serious, less conversational, and suddenly Zoe realized why.

"You think I have a gift, don't you?" Zoe asked. "The women in our family acquire their gift around the age I am now, so you think it's going to show up."

"I think it already has."

"Why? Because of Cornelius? You told me women with lineage in Everlasting can usually see him. My seeing him doesn't prove anything more than you seeing him does."

"It's not Cornelius. It's the weather."

"What about it?" Maybe that hit on the head that Sapphire had taken had done more damage than they thought.

"You haven't noticed the odd things happening with the weather? Think about it. The night you arrived the forecast was completely clear yet a thunderstorm appeared out of nowhere. The same thing happened right after your frustrating conversation with Deputy February. Then there was the hail. Even if you want to dismiss the first two as flukes, you of all people know better than to dismiss that hailstorm."

Zoe stared. "You think I made those things

happen? That somehow I can influence the weather?"

"When I was talking to people today, I checked. That hail only fell on my property. No one else saw even a tiny sliver of ice."

Zoe shook her head, afraid to say anything. Afraid of the uneasy feeling in her stomach.

"You've always been fascinated with the weather," Sapphire said. "Even when you were a child, you'd beg your parents to let you stand in the garage and watch the storms blow in. You've made it your life's work. Even before you started coming into your gift, there was something inside you that knew."

Zoe looked out the windshield at the clear blue sky. It wasn't possible and yet somehow, she knew what her aunt said was the truth.

"You're saying that if I figure out how to control it, I could whip up a storm sitting here in this parking lot?"

"I'm not sure."

"But you just said—"

"I think you influence the weather, but I don't know how far that influence extends. Cats outside of Everlasting don't understand me, and I don't feel anything from them."

"Why would that be?"

Sapphire shrugged. "I don't know. Maybe because of the emerald. Maybe the power of that stone is what makes everything in Everlasting possible but its reach only goes so far."

"I—I just—"

Zoe stopped talking when she saw Monte's truck pull around the corner of the parking lot and head their way. It was probably just as well. She needed some time to think about everything Sapphire had said.

"What's that in the back of his truck?" Sapphire asked.

Zoe leaned forward and squinted. "It looks like crates."

When Monte pulled up next to her, she could clearly see the wooden crates with the name of an appliance manufacturer stamped on the side.

"Your kitchen appliances were delivered today," Zoe said. "That must be the crates they came in. But surely he doesn't expect us to ride in those things back to the lighthouse."

"It's not a bad idea, really. At least as not looking suspicious."

Zoe climbed out of the car and gave Monte and Sam a wave as she walked over to his truck. Monte pointed to the crates.

"Pretty smart, huh?" Monte asked.

"If you like bouncing around on a block of wood," Zoe said.

"Oh, Dane took care of that. We lined the

bottoms with the cushions from Sapphire's outdoor furniture."

"Come on," Sapphire said, and climbed into the back of the truck. "It will be an adventure."

"Says the woman who does yoga." Zoe sighed and followed Sapphire into the truck. Monte and Sam joined them and removed the side panels from the two crates.

Zoe leaned down to check it out. It wasn't horribly small and there were two cushions on the bottom. She could probably sit cross-legged on one and use the other for her back. Still, it was a good thing neither of them were claustrophobic. The crates had tiny narrow cracks between the slats of wood that would allow in some light, but basically, they were going to be closed in a small box.

"Age before beauty," Sapphire said and crawled inside the box, positioning the cushions exactly as Zoe had figured she would. Once she was seated, she gave Monte a thumbs-up and they attached the panel to the front of the crate.

Zoe shook her head and crawled inside the box. It took her several seconds to get positioned, then Monte and Sam closed her up and she sat in semi-darkness wondering where things had gone so wrong. Last week, if anyone had told her she'd be locked in a crate on the back of a pickup truck, contemplating her supposed ability to control the weather, while waiting to perform a takedown of criminals with her ex-lover, she would have asked what they were smoking.

But here she was.

Everlasting proving once again that truth was stranger than fiction.

The unloading process proved a bit more difficult than the loading. Dane had Monte pull his truck around to the back of the lighthouse, then the three men managed to lift the crates off the back of the truck and onto the ground. There was a slight drop right there at the end and Zoe was thankful for the cushions. Then she was tilted sideways onto a dolly and wheeled into the lighthouse.

Sapphire was already bent over touching her toes when Zoe crawled out of her crate and rose to a standing position, probably with far less grace than her aunt had managed. Monte and Sam were both grinning at them like they'd reeled in the catch of the day, and Zoe couldn't help but smile back at them. The past twenty-four hours were probably the most exciting they'd had in years.

"Are you all right?" Dane asked.

"Fantastic," Sapphire said. "I meditated on the way here, and now I'm relaxed and ready for a power nap."

"I ate two cinnamon rolls on the way," Zoe said, "so I'm ready for a power nap as well."

Dane smiled. "I was afraid you might be mad about the unorthodox travel arrangements."

She shrugged. "It was clever. If the thieves were watching, there's no way they would have guessed. That's all that matters."

Sapphire went over to Monte and Sam and gave them each a hug and kiss on the cheek. The old fishermen looked pleased and just a little embarrassed.

"Thank you for helping with this," she said. "If you all don't mind, I'm going to head upstairs for a hot shower and some rest."

"I should get upstairs as well," Zoe said. "Thank you guys. I owe you a beer."

"Make it a whiskey," Monte said, "and you've got a deal."

"Whiskey it is," Zoe said.

"Do you need me to bring anything upstairs for you?"

Zoe shook her head. The last thing she wanted was Dane in her bedroom. She'd just spent thirty minutes closed in a box with nothing but the cinnamon rolls and her own thoughts, several featuring the man in front of her. What she needed was more space and less noise to try to make sense of them all.

"If you could just grab me a soda from the fridge," she said, "I'll take it up with me."

"A bottled water for me," Sapphire said.

Dane retrieved the drinks and the two of them headed up the stairs. They stopped on the landing at Zoe's room, and Sapphire studied her for a couple seconds, then hugged her.

"You look like you needed it," Sapphire said. "I know things are weighing heavy on you. I can see it in your eyes. I can feel the burden you bear like it's my own. But the decisions you have to make are ones I can't help you with. They have to come from your heart and not the desires of an old woman. I love you, Zoe. And all I've ever wanted was for you to be happy."

Zoe's chest constricted and she kissed her aunt on the cheek. "I love you too."

Sapphire nodded and headed upstairs. Zoe watched until she rounded the stairs and went out of sight before going into her bedroom and closing the door behind her. First, she would take a long hot shower to loosen up her back and neck. Then she planned on crawling into bed and thinking about her life until they were stiff again.

She gave it five minutes, tops.

TWO HOURS LATER, Zoe sat cross-legged on the bed, her laptop in front of her. She read the email one more time before moving the pointer to the Send button. She hesitated, biting her lip. This was it. This one click would change not just her entire life but her entire life's plan. It would erase six years of hard work with the first sentence.

Consider this notice of my resignation.

She tapped her finger once on the track pad and flopped back against the pillows she'd stacked up behind her. She closed her eyes and waited for the horror of what she'd done to hit her, but instead of the intense regret and overwhelming what-have-I-done feeling that she expected, she felt only one thing.

Relief.

And what does that tell you?

She knew the answer but it was hard to admit that she'd made a mistake. That the one thing she'd thought would make her happy, wouldn't. That the city she'd thought she'd love, she hadn't. The truth was, she'd been pursuing the job with such a single-minded focus that she'd never stopped to consider whether she still should. As for LA, she was certain it was perfect for some people. Just not for her.

She'd been there six years and didn't have a single person she could honestly call a friend. Plenty of acquaintances, but no one she confided in. She'd been to the beach exactly four times, and two of them were for her job. She couldn't afford a bunch of designer items, so the shopping wasn't a draw, and even though the die-hards loved California for the weather, she actually missed the cold. Sure, it was a horrible pain in the rear to shovel drives and maneuver vehicles on ice, but that first snow of the season was always so beautiful. That light blanket of white covering everything in sight, casting the entire town in a different light.

And then there was the pull of Everlasting.

She hadn't wanted to admit it, but ever since she'd looked up at the lighthouse that first night, she'd had the overwhelming feeling of belonging. That this was her place. She knew that nostalgia and love for Sapphire were a big part of her feelings, but the core sense of rightness went so much deeper than that.

And then there was Dane. She'd thought time would erase her feelings, but it had only hidden them from her conscious mind. But her love for him had still resided deep inside, just waiting for the right time to bubble up. In LA she'd managed to keep it at bay, but returning to Everlasting was the only catalyst it needed to leak out into her consciousness. When he'd kissed her, she thought it meant he'd felt the same, but she couldn't be certain. It might have been familiarity that had drawn him to her during an emotionally charged moment. Which meant that regardless of her feelings for him, Dane wasn't necessarily a part of her future.

So, taking stock, she currently had no job and no man, but she had a place to live and her aunt contending Zoe had the magical ability to influence the weather. If nothing turned up on the job front, she could always fall back on charging farmers for bringing rain. Given that she could be working with limited range, she might not make enough to fund a 401(k), but she could probably keep Sapphire in the ingredients for baked goods. On the plus side of things, despite LA's high cost of living, she had quite a bit of savings—probably because she'd done more working than living. And since her apartment was so small, she didn't have a lot of things to pack.

She blew out a breath. Closing in on thirty, single, unemployed, and living with her aunt and ten cats. She'd become a collection of walking stereotypes.

But at the moment, none of that mattered. Right now, the only important thing was catching the thieves. She could figure the rest of it out later… when all she had was time.

Chapter Sixteen

_____

"You can come down now," Dane called from the bottom of the stairs.

Zoe and Sapphire had been waiting for his call on the second-floor landing. It was the end of his official workday, and he was securing the lighthouse, which meant closing the blinds and drawing the drapes. Now they could go downstairs without worrying that someone would see them.

When they reached the first floor, Zoe gasped and moved out of the way for Sapphire to see her kitchen. The backsplash still needed to be installed, but the white Carrara marble countertops were so beautiful against the soft green cabinets that Zoe couldn't believe it was the same old brown kitchen that had been here before.

"It's gorgeous," Sapphire said, moving forward to run her hands along the counter. "When you showed me the materials, I knew it was going to be, but it's so much more than I even thought it would be."

"Wait until I get the backsplash done," Dane said.

"I'm definitely sleeping down here then," Sapphire said. "Or maybe I'll just skip the sleeping and spend all night baking."

Dane smiled. "Let me get it finished, then you can go all nocturnal."

"Speaking of nocturnal activities," Zoe said, anxious to get on with the plan and get things back to normal.

Dane went into the laundry room and returned with a rifle. "I had Monte and Sam pick this up from my house earlier. You were a good shot with skeet," he said to Zoe. "I don't suppose you've done much shooting in California, though."

Zoe took the rifle from him. "No, but I haven't forgotten how. Besides, all I should have to do is point. I'm sorta hoping to avoid any actual shooting."

"Me too," Dane agreed. "But we need a big enough threat to keep them in place and this should do it. The sun is going to set in about twenty minutes, so I'm going to head home. It should be dark by the time I get back. I'll use the shoreline to come back and approach the lighthouse from the beach. I turned the front porch light on but intentionally left the back one off. It's cloudy so I should be able to get back inside without being seen."

Dane's cell phone rang and he checked the display. "It's Monte."

He answered the call and frowned. When he hung up, he looked over at them. "Monte said the Belmont brothers were in the bar this afternoon and Frank Belmont had a black eye. Sam asked him what the other guy looked like and he just scowled at him."

"It was the hail," Sapphire said.

"Are they still there?" Zoe asked.

"Yeah, they're playing pool, but the game's almost done."

Zoe nodded. "Get going. We'll be fine. They're not going to head this way until it's dark. Someone might see their truck and report it."

"I'll call as soon as I get on the walkway to the lighthouse. Be ready to let me in." Dane headed out the back door.

Sapphire looked over at Zoe. "I guess we can't move the refrigerator until Dane gets back."

"You don't need to be moving refrigerators anyway."

"It's got wheels. Besides, we need something to do. We can't just stand here watching the door for the next thirty minutes."

"Fine, so we'll have a Danish in your new

kitchen and then watch the back door for twenty minutes."

"I'll make coffee."

"Eighteen minutes."

Sapphire laughed. "I've really missed you, Zoe. Please don't wait so long to come visit again or I might fake another fall."

"About that…I was thinking of staying a while."

"Really? That would be wonderful! How long? A week? Two?"

"I'm not really sure. As long as it will take me to find a job and my own place and—"

Sapphire rushed forward and grabbed Zoe in a hug, twirling them both around. Finally, she stopped spinning and looked at Zoe with a grin that practically split her face.

"You're coming home," Sapphire said. "I can't tell you how happy that makes me. You belong here, Zoe, but it had to be your decision. And no talk of getting your own place. The lighthouse is your home."

Zoe shook her head. "You have your own life and routine here. I don't want to interfere with that."

"You wouldn't be interfering at all. You'd be completing the last piece of a puzzle. The lighthouse is yours, Zoe. It always has been but if it makes you feel better, I made it official years ago when I made my will. I left everything to you."

"But Dad…"

"Your parents have no interest in returning to Everlasting, and they never wanted to live in the lighthouse. They prefer to live within walking distance of restaurants and stores. You know remote living was never their thing."

Zoe nodded, unable to speak for fear of starting to cry. And if she started, she wasn't sure she'd be able to stop. Sapphire had left her the lighthouse. She'd always figured her dad would inherit it or maybe Sapphire would leave it to the town with the stipulation that it become a historical landmark. Zoe never considered that the one place she'd always felt she belonged would become her home.

"I have my doubts you'll be here for long anyway," Sapphire said. "I predict that before long you'll be living in an adorable bungalow just down the shore."

Zoe shook her head. "I'm not ready to go there and I don't think he is either."

"Doesn't matter. I saw the two of you then and I see you now, and what's between you hasn't diminished. It's never going to."

"I guess we'll see. Now, let's have that Danish."

Sapphire stared at her for several seconds, then hugged her again before bouncing across the kitchen like a child at a carnival. Zoe couldn't help but smile. There was no one in the world like her aunt, and Zoe was just happy she'd come to her senses while Sapphire was still around. She could have lost her when she fell, but instead of losing anything, she'd found herself.

THEY ALL SAT at the kitchen island, looking at the clock every minute. They were three pots of coffee and one six-pack of diet soda into the night, and it was getting longer with every passing silent second. Periodically, Cornelius would pop inside and let them know he was still patrolling and still hadn't seen anything. It was close to midnight and despite the nap she'd taken earlier, Zoe was starting to grow weary. But in all fairness, she'd had a big day already.

"Maybe they didn't find out we were going to be out of town," Sapphire said.

Zoe shook her head. "People in Canada know we're supposed to be out of town. Maybe they changed their mind."

Dane sighed. "Anything is possible, but I can't believe their intentions would change so drastically from one night to the next."

"Monte is certain they left the bar at eight?" Zoe asked.

"He followed them out and saw them leave," Dane said.

"Maybe they had another job to do before this

one," Sapphire said. "I mean, they haven't been caught yet, right, so what if they had something planned for tonight before they found out we weren't going to be here? Something that had to be done earlier because the people who lived there were only going to be gone for dinner or a movie or something. They think they'll have all night in here."

"Yes, but they don't know what they're looking for," Zoe pointed out. "And if it's the last robbery they'd ever have to do, assuming they find the emerald, wouldn't they concentrate effort on the job that leads to instant retirement?"

"You're probably right," Sapphire said. "I wouldn't make a good criminal at all. So many things to take into account."

"Most criminals don't make good criminals," Dane said. "That's why they get caught."

"Well, these might prove that theory wrong," Zoe said. "Either that or they got drunk somewhere else or in a fight somewhere else or a wreck driving drunk." She sighed. "How many nights are we going to have to do this?"

"As many as it takes," Dane said.

"Maybe Sapphire could just get a big rottweiler," Zoe said.

"I think the cats would vote that one down," Sapphire said.

"I suppose a pet tiger is out of the question?" Zoe asked. "Can you talk to big cats?"

"I don't know," Sapphire said. "I've never had the opportunity, but it's an interesting thought."

"Before anyone starts playing Dr. Dolittle," Dane said, "let's give this a few tries."

"If we were vampires, this wouldn't be a problem," Sapphire said.

"If we were vampires," Zoe said, "we'd be dead and all of this would be moot."

"True," Sapphire said, "but—"

"He's coming!" Cornelius burst through the wall and ran into the kitchen. "He's creeping out of the woods now, headed for the front door."

Zoe repeated what he said for Dane.

"Only one man?" Dane asked.

"Yes," Cornelius said.

Zoe nodded.

"Keep us updated," Dane said. "Everyone in position."

Zoe and Sapphire hurried upstairs and Zoe grabbed the rifle from her room and crept back down the stairs, stopping where the bend would have exposed her to the living room. Sapphire stayed behind on the landing, ready with her cell phone and the army of cats behind her. Dane had headed for his spot on the side of the cabinet, where he would be hidden from anyone entering through the front door. Now all Zoe had to do was wait for

Dane to give the signal, then block the thief from going up the stairs.

She took in a breath and slowly let it out, trying to slow her racing pulse. Calm was good. Calm was steady. She just had to keep reminding herself of that. Straining, she tried to make out noise from downstairs, but the only sound she heard was the wind whistling through the trees.

"He's opening the door!" Cornelius yelled. "Still only one man."

Zoe frowned. The second man had run because of the cats that first night. Maybe he had refused to come inside again. He might be waiting in the truck, playing the getaway driver, and had probably been the one to call her from the hospital the night before.

She heard the door open and prepared for what was coming next.

Cornelius' voice sounded through the light-house. "He's inside!"

Chapter Seventeen

Zoe clenched the rifle so tightly her hands started to ache. Every second seemed like an hour but finally she heard Dane's voice.

"Stop or I'll shoot!"

She ran down the stairs and aimed her rifle at the masked man standing in the middle of the living room, looking back at Dane, who stood in the front doorway, blocking his access. When the stairs creaked, the man whirled around, his eyes widening when he saw Zoe on the stairs with a rifle. He glanced to the side but the refrigerator blocking the back door completely eliminated it as an option.

Cornelius stood a couple of feet from the man, clapping and cheering.

"Drop the rifle." A man's voice sounded across the room and Zoe looked past the thief to see a masked man standing behind Dane. "I can shoot you and your girlfriend before you get that rifle swung around," he said. "Drop it now."

"Oh my God!" Cornelius yelled. "Send down the cats! Sapphire! Unleash the beasts!"

Dane sat the butt of the rifle on the floor and let it drop.

"You too, Annie Oakley," the man said, and nodded at Zoe. "On the floor in front of you."

Zoe heard the stampede coming behind her as she dropped the rifle onto the rug. She leaned against the wall as the cats came running by at breakneck speed. They skidded off the stairs and made a beeline for the front door.

"Hell no!" the man with the pistol yelled and shoved Dane, sending him tumbling over an accent table. "Get out of there," he screamed at his partner.

The man with the pistol whirled around and sped out of the lighthouse, the cats and Cornelius close behind. The first thief attempted to run through the front door, but Dane launched forward from the floor and tackled him at the knees.

Cornelius, who'd run outside after the other thief, barreled back through the front of the lighthouse screaming. "He's going to shoot the cats!"

"Not my babies!" Sapphire yelled. "Zoe, use your gift. Do something."

Zoe ran out the front door and saw the man on the drive, leveling his pistol at the herd of running cats. Something at her core started to burn and she felt a rush of energy course through her almost like an electrical current.

A second later, a bolt of lightning burst from the sky and struck the thief, throwing him on the ground, steam coming off the pistol. Sapphire ran up behind her.

"Are they all right?" she asked. "Are my babies okay?"

"They're all good," Zoe said, still unable to believe what had just happened.

"Is he dead?" Cornelius asked.

"Do you care?" Sapphire asked. "Trying to shoot my babies."

Zoe looked over at Dane, who had just finished tying up the first thief and left him sitting on the living room floor, slumped against the couch. He didn't appear to have any fight left in him.

"I'm going for the other one," Dane said, and headed outside with his rifle and more rope.

Zoe stomped into the living room and yanked the mask off his head, ready to level her fist at Frank Belmont, and stared in shock as Dr. Prescott looked up at her. Sapphire stepped up beside her, looking as bewildered as Zoe felt.

"Why?" Sapphire asked. "Why would you do this to me?"

"I need the emerald," he said. "It's my only hope."

The cancer.

"You're dying, aren't you?" Zoe asked.

Dr. Prescott nodded.

"How long?"

"A couple of months," he said. "Maybe more."

Suddenly, it all made sense. It was Dr. Prescott who'd prescribed the sleeping pills for Sapphire, thinking she'd be out cold when he broke in. It was Dr. Prescott who'd kept her in the hospital longer than Mary Jo had expected, planning to lure Zoe out of the lighthouse. But how a doctor could believe in cure by magic emerald, she had no idea.

Before Zoe could open her mouth to ask any one of the hundred questions that came to mind, she heard Dane yelling for them to come outside. As they exited the lighthouse, the cats began to stroll back in, looking incredibly pleased with themselves. Zoe and Sapphire hurried over to Dane, who stood over the second thief.

"You're not going to believe this," Dane said and pointed down at the now-exposed face of the other man.

Deputy February.

"Is he dead?" Zoe asked, her voice shaking. She wanted February to pay for what he'd done to Sapphire, but she didn't want to be responsible for killing someone.

"Unconscious," Dane said. "And his gun is completely melted."

Sapphire looked down at the deputy, then threw her hands in the air. "The whole world has gone crazy. The other man is Dr. Prescott."

"Your doctor?" Dane stared at them in surprise. "What the hell is going on in this town?"

"I don't know but after I call the sheriff, I'm calling the state police," Zoe said. "Clearly there needs to be some calendar sorting down at the sheriff's department, and I don't know the rules on Sheriff Bull arresting one of her own deputies."

Dane nodded. "Probably a good idea."

Zoe pulled out her cell phone and called the sheriff's department and the state police, explaining that she had apprehended two intruders in her aunt's house and one of them was local law enforcement. Dispatch at the sheriff's department said they'd roust Sheriff Bull out of bed and get her over there. The state police had an off-duty in town for the festival and said he would be there in fifteen minutes. She also asked them to dispatch paramedics to the scene as one of the intruders had been struck by lightning.

She stuck the phone back in her pocket and looked at Dane and Sapphire.

"I am so confused," she said. "But the good news is this is over."

ZOE SAT on a huge rock at the end of the beach path and looked out over the ocean. The wind blowing across the water was chilly, so she zipped her jacket and pulled the hoodie over her head. The cold didn't at all detract from the beauty.

And now, you can see this every day.

That thought made her smile, and that in itself was huge because when she'd left Everlasting, she'd believed the only thing that could make her happy was to never be back. Now she couldn't imagine herself anywhere else. Maybe she'd had to leave before she could realize that she belonged here. That Everlasting was where her future was, even though she had no idea what that future held.

She was still processing the events of the night before and had yet to reconcile Dr. Prescott and Deputy February as the bad guys. In a way, she understood Dr. Prescott's reasons, at least on an emotional level. He was dying and desperate, and given Sapphire's incredible health for her age, he thought she held the secret that he needed to cure himself. He'd begged her forgiveness before the state police arrived, and even though Zoe was still angry at him for putting Sapphire at risk, she couldn't help feeling a little sorry for him.

As for February, she had no idea why the detective had taken up with Prescott. He hadn't regained consciousness by the time the paramedics arrived and the state police had accompanied them to the hospital. The police had spent a couple hours taking their statements, and then admonished them against similar action in the future as they had gotten lucky that no one was hurt except one of the bad guys.

The statements hadn't included any mention of Zoe's summoning the lightning, of course. Dane was completely in the dark about her newfound skill set, although she was sure he knew something had changed. But she wanted to talk to him about all of it—the weather, her resignation, her feelings for him —when everything had settled down. Last night definitely hadn't been the right time. When the police were done, they'd all been exhausted and more than happy to go straight to bed. The next day was going to be a busy one because as soon as word got out, Zoe had no doubt that a constant stream of visitors and phone calls would be in her aunt's future.

She'd been right. Dane had dropped by that morning to see how they were doing and said he was going to check in with the police and he'd be back that afternoon, hopefully with an update on everything. By 9:00 a.m. the phone started ringing, and at 11:00 a.m. the first visitor arrived. A group of four women from Sapphire's yoga class had shown up about fifteen minutes ago, and Zoe had taken the opportunity to step out and find a quiet place to decompress. It had been an extraordinary night and an excitable day, and she just needed to get away from the hum of voices for a while.

"I take it you are escaping the yoga club excitement?" Dane's voice sounded behind her.

She turned to see him step off the path and he took a seat on the rock next to her.

"After the tenth telling," Zoe said, "I got a little bored. I thought a little peace and quiet was in order."

"I didn't mean to disrupt your peace."

"You didn't. Besides, I want to know what you found out. Is February awake? Did he say anything?"

"Awake and singing like a bird, not that it matters. His excuse isn't nearly as compelling as the doctor's."

"This ought to be good."

"Money. Good old-fashioned green. But the reason he was desperate for the money is one I haven't heard before. He said Sheriff Bull wants to marry him and he needed the money to get away."

"Seriously? Do you think he's telling the truth?"

"Who knows? Dr. Prescott has been treating him for anxiety, which is how they hooked up, so I'm guessing the good doctor could confirm February's claim if it came to that. But it doesn't matter."

"Why's that?"

"The state police are bringing them both up on breaking-and-entering charges and assault for what happened to Sapphire and for shoving me. I don't think he will serve a lot of time but as a cop, anything February serves will be unpleasant. He'll probably plead out if they offer him anything less than what he'd likely get at a sentencing. It's doubtful Prescott will even make it *to* jail, much less out."

"I wonder how they found out about the emerald to begin with."

"Oh, I know that too. February said Mary Jo told Prescott the story after that dinner, probably just relaying an interesting tidbit that she'd heard, and he verified it with September. I'm sure she wouldn't have repeated it if she'd known the doctor would go off the rails."

"I'm sure. She's probably going to feel bad now. I'll have to go talk to her about that. You know, I feel sorry for Prescott, despite what he did. I don't think he meant for Sapphire to get hurt."

"I don't either, but he had a choice. He could have asked Sapphire to help him find the emerald."

"I don't think she would have," Zoe said. "Not for the reasons he wanted it. Sapphire believes the emerald is what created the magic in Everlasting and that if it's removed, the magic might disappear along with it. She would never let an individual with his own agenda gain possession of the stone."

"True."

"I'm afraid now that all this is big news, more

people will try to find the stone, and we have nothing to give them to keep them away."

"That's not exactly true. Based on my statement last night, the state police had a chat with Harriet Wilson about their concern that she and Sapphire could be targets for people looking for the stone."

"I bet that went over well."

Dane grinned. "She called them a bunch of damned fools and said no one could find the emerald because it doesn't exist anymore. Apparently, in another one of her journals, one of her ancestors wrote about how they cast a spell to crush the emerald into powder and sprinkled it on the ground all over the area."

"Why didn't she tell me that when I was there?"

"The state police asked the same thing. She said because you didn't ask and it wasn't any of your damned business anyway."

"Why am I not surprised?"

"The good news is, she's agreed to let the local newspaper make copies of the journals and write up the story of the emerald. So hopefully, everyone will get the word that it's dust that disappeared in the soil of Everlasting many, many years ago."

"And you believe all of that?"

Dane shook his head. "It's as good a theory as anything else in this town. There's always been odd things...stuff I couldn't explain but knew to exist. I tried not to dwell on it because I knew there weren't any answers other than blind acceptance of something that isn't supposed to exist. Then I come face-to-face, so to speak, with a ghost and see you force lightning from the sky."

Zoe looked down at the sand. "You caught that, huh?"

"It was hard to miss with Sapphire telling you to use your gift, then lightning appearing out of nowhere and striking February's gun. That's either deliberate or the biggest coincidence that has ever occurred."

"I haven't wrapped my head around it yet," Zoe said. "I mean, I believe there's something not normal at play. I felt something inside when that lightning came and somehow I knew I was the cause. But that's all I am sure about. Everything else, well, I guess it's as big an unknown as the rest of my life."

"What are you talking about?"

She turned to look at him so that she could gauge his reaction. "I resigned from my job. I'm going to move back to Everlasting and live with Sapphire and try to figure it all out, hopefully without injuring someone else with lightning or hail or a random hurricane."

"You're moving home?" His tone was a mixture of hope and disbelief.

"Yes. I suppose this is where you get to tell me 'I told you so.'"

He frowned. "There's no victory in being right when it hurts you. I know how badly you wanted that job. It's everything you ever dreamed of. What happened?"

"A lot of things. And all of them made it clear that I'd been pursuing the wrong thing all along. That promotion wasn't going to make me happy. Living in LA was boring at best, but mostly miserable. It wasn't my place. Everlasting is."

"What are you going to do?"

"I'm not sure yet, but there's an idea rolling around in my head."

"What's that?"

"The corporation that owns the local radio station is looking to sell."

"The station with the weather forecaster who is wrong more than he's right?"

"Well, in his defense, everything he learned about meteorology is out of books from Noah's ark. The corporation said he's making noise about retiring. Maybe a new owner would give him that final push."

Dane's eyes widened. "You're thinking about buying the radio station?"

"Why not? I have some savings, and the corporation said they'd finance the rest. This is all very loose talk over a thirty-minute phone call, but it could turn into something."

"I think that would be incredible. I think *you* would be incredible."

"It wouldn't be cheating?"

"What do you mean?"

She smiled. "Well, it's not exactly forecasting if I can change the weather when I'm wrong."

"I have a feeling it won't be that easy."

"Probably not."

"Is the job the only reason you changed your mind about living here?"

She shrugged. "There's this guy. He's stubborn and never admits when he's wrong, but he's got an eye for custom finishes and a big heart. I guess I was hoping there was still room in it for me."

Dane put his hands on both sides of her face and looked her directly in her eyes. "That room has been empty and waiting for you all this time."

"Then maybe it's time to redecorate it and move back in."

THE END

Newsletter

Sign up for Jana's Newsletter at
http://janadeleon.com/

About the Author

Jana DeLeon was raised in southwest Louisiana among the bayous and gators. Her hometown is Carlyss, but you probably won't find it on a map. Jana has never stumbled across a mystery or a ghost like her heroines, but she's still hopeful. She now resides in Dallas, Texas with her husband and the most spoiled Sheltie in the world.

To learn more, check out Jana's website.

www.janadeleon.com

Featured Titles from Jana Deleon

Reading order for humorous series books:

The Miss Fortune Series

Louisiana Longshot

Lethal Bayou Beauty

Swamp Sniper

Swamp Team 3

Gator Bait

Soldiers of Fortune

Shaye Archer Series

Malevolent

The Ghost-in-Law Series

Trouble in Mudbug

Mischief in Mudbug

Featured Titles from Jana Deleon

Showdown in Mudbug
Resurrection in Mudbug
Missing in Mudbug
Chaos in Mudbug
Rose and Helena Save Christmas (novella)
The Helena Diaries: Trouble in Mudbug
(companion novella to Trouble in Mudbug)

Note: You should read Trouble in Mudbug before reading The Helena Diaries as it contains spoilers.

Standalone Books
Rumble on the Bayou
Unlucky

More Everlasting...

COZY PARANORMAL MYSTERY ROMANCE NOVELS

The Happily Everlasting Series

Dead Man Talking
by Jana DeLeon

Once Hunted, Twice Shy
by Mandy M. Roth

Fooled Around and Spelled in Love
by Michelle M. Pillow

Witchful Thinking
by Kristen Painter

Visit Everlasting
https://welcometoeverlasting.com/

Dead Man Talking

by Jana DeLeon

Welcome to Everlasting, Maine, where there's no such thing as normal.

Meteorologist Zoe Parker put Everlasting in her rearview mirror as soon as she had her college degree in hand. But when Sapphire, her eccentric great-aunt, takes a tumble down the stairs in her lighthouse home, Zoe returns to the tiny fishing hamlet to look after her. Zoe has barely crossed the county line when strange things start happening with the weather, and she discovers Sapphire's fall was no accident. Someone is searching the lighthouse but Sapphire has no idea what they're looking for. Determined to ensure her aunt's ongoing safety, Zoe promises to expose the intruders, even though it means staying in Everlasting and confronting the past she thought she'd put behind her.

Dane Stanton never expected to see Zoe standing in the middle of her aunt's living room, and was even more unprepared for the flood of emotion he experiences when coming face to face with his old flame. Zoe is just as independent and determined as he remembered, and Dane knows she won't rest until Sapphire can return to the lighthouse in peace, so he offers to help her sort things out.

Armed with old legends, Sapphire's ten cats, and a talking ghost, Zoe has to reconcile her feelings for Dane and embrace her destiny before it's too late.

Once Hunted, Twice Shy

by Mandy M. Roth

Welcome to Everlasting, Maine, where there's no such thing as normal.

Wolf shifter Hugh Lupine simply wants to make it through the month and win the bet he has with his best friend. He's not looking to date anyone, or to solve a murder, but when a breath taking beauty runs him over (literally) he's left no choice but to take notice of the quirky, sassy newcomer. She'd be perfect if it wasn't for the fact she's the grand-daughter of the local supernatural hunter. Even if he can set aside his feelings about her family, Pene-lope is his complete opposite in all ways.

Penelope Messing wanted to get away from the harsh reminder that her boyfriend of two years dumped her. Several pints of ice cream and one plane ticket to Maine later, she's ready to forget her troubles. At least for a bit. When she arrives in the sleepy little fishing town of Everlasting, for a surprise visit with her grandfather, she soon learns that outrunning one problem can lead to a whole mess of others. She finds herself the prime suspect in a double homicide. She doesn't even kill spiders, let alone people, but local law enforcement has their eyes on her.

The secrets of Everlasting come to light and Penelope has to not only accept that things that go bump in the night are real, but apparently, she's destined for a man who sprouts fur and has a bizarre obsession with fish sticks. Can they clear Penelope's name and set aside their differences to find true love?

Fooled Around and Spelled in Love

by Michelle M. Pillow

Welcome to Everlasting, Maine, where there's no such thing as normal.

Anna Crawford is well aware her town is filled with supernaturals, but she isn't exactly willing to embrace her paranormal gifts. Her aunt says she's a witch-in-denial. All Anna wants is to live a quiet "normal" life and run her business, Witch's Brew Coffee Shop and Bakery. But everything is about to be turned upside down the moment Jackson Argent walks into her life.

Jackson isn't sure why he agreed to come back to his boyhood home of Everlasting. It's like a spell was cast and he couldn't say no. Covering the Cranberry Festival isn't exactly the hard-hitting news this reporter is used to. But when a local death is ruled an accident, and the police aren't interested in investigating, he takes it upon himself to get to the bottom of the mystery. To do that, he'll need to enlist the help of the beautiful coffee shop owner.

It soon becomes apparent things are not what they seem and more than coffee is brewing in Everlasting.

Witchful Thinking

by Kristen Painter

*Welcome to Everlasting, Maine, where there's no such thing
as normal.*

Charlotte Fenchurch knows that, which is why she's
not that surprised when a very special book of
magic falls into her hands at the library where she
works. As a fledgling witch, owning her own
grimoire is a dream come true. But there's something...mysterious about the book she just can't
figure out.

Leopard shifter Walker Black knows what's odd
about the book. It's full of black magic and so
dangerous that it could destroy the world. Good
thing the Fraternal Order of Light has sent him to
Everlasting to recover it and put it into safe storage.

If he has to, he'll even take the witch who owns it into custody.

That is until he meets Charlotte and realizes she's not out to watch the world burn. She's sweet and kind and wonderful. Suddenly protecting her is all he wants to do. Well, that and kiss her some more. But dark forces seem determined to get their hands on the book, making Charlotte their target, and Walker worries that he won't be able to protect her from them – or the organization he works for.

Can Walker and Charlotte survive the onslaught of danger? Or is that just witchful thinking?

Visit Everlasting

https://welcometoeverlasting.com/

Made in the USA
Lexington, KY
14 October 2017